GEMINI

ACADEMY

JESSIE PADDOCK

Scholastic Inc.

ISBN 978-1-338-28082-1

10 9 8 7 6 5 4 3 2 1   18 19 20 21 22

Printed in China   68
First edition, September 2018

Book design by Maeve Norton

FOR HAM

CHAPTER ONE

GLORIA

Gloria Garcia hadn't felt like herself for a while now. Two months, two weeks, and two days, if you want to get technical about it. She couldn't quite put her finger on it, but something was definitely . . . off. Gloria had lost her taste for nutritious vegetables, she no longer saw the point of making her bed (she was just going to mess it up at night anyway), and she had started to wonder just how far good manners would get her in life. In short, Gloria had been struggling to look at things on the bright side. For a Sun Twin at Gemini Academy—the premiere boarding school in the world for twins—this was as un-Sun Twin as she could be. And after seven years at the academy, Gloria certainly knew better.

But she couldn't help it.

Gloria had never before doubted that she fit in at Sun School, where Sun Twins studied the virtues of being model citizens of the world. She was the Sun Class President, after all. But after these past two months, two weeks, and two days, she wasn't so sure anymore. It was just a feeling she had—a feeling she hoped would go away as swiftly as it had arrived. Maybe she'd talk to her sister, Greta, about it later.

Maybe.

On that particularly pensive Friday morning, Ms. Heart rambled on about kitten quilts during Inspirational Art class.

"Excellent work, everyone. You are all doing a magnificent job. I am feeling such joy at the promise of the quilt already!" Ms. Heart praised.

Gloria sat at her desk and stared out at the tall oak tree that stood on the perfectly manicured lawn, imagining what it would be like to be . . . a chipmunk. As far as Gloria could tell, it seemed great. After two solid weeks of chipmunk watching, Gloria had come to several important chipmunk conclusions.

One, chipmunks had awesome hair. Or fur. Or whatever. Gloria just knew that the sweet black-and-white stripe would look so cute in her own cinnamon-colored hair. But, of course, after one Moon Twin (that's what the good Sun Twins called their bad-twin counterparts) had been caught dying a stripe in her locks—totally *not* chipmunk inspired, by the way—all twins were forbidden from dying their hair any color ever.

Ugh.

So. Many. Rules.

Two, and more important, chipmunks were stellar hoarders. They could stockpile, from what Gloria could see, dozens of nuts in their ever-expanding cheeks. Such a cool trick! The only thing Sun School teachers at Gemini Academy ever talked about were the virtues of sharing. After watching this dynamic little chipmunk keep all those nuts for itself, Gloria wondered what it would be like to keep something just for herself, too.

Three—and perhaps most important—chipmunks were great burrowers. If Gloria had the ability to dig secret tunnels all through Gemini's campus, the question was not where she would burrow, but where *wouldn't* she burrow? There'd be no stopping her. Gloria would be able to spy on anyone and everyone; she'd burrow and sneak where no Sun Twin or Moon Twin had gone before.

Oh, and PS, chipmunks communicate through chirps. That was a fact Gloria had looked up, but it was maybe the thing she envied most. If she could communicate with Greta using sounds that nobody else understood, then maybe they could arrange more than one secret meet-up per week.

But truth be told, Gloria didn't really care all that much about chipmunks. She'd just watched them a lot during Inspirational Art class. These days, Gloria found Inspirational Art class insufferably boring. Ms. Heart insisted they spend a solid week working on their kitten-themed embroidery patches, then *another* week perfectly sewing the individual kitten squares together into an enormous quilt. The goal was to make a giant, perfect kitten-themed quilt that would be extra kitten-y and extra perfect as the centerpiece for the upcoming Gemini Academy Fair. (Obviously, they would then donate the blanket to a local nursing home.) One week into the mind-numbing project and Gloria was ready to give up. Or become a chipmunk. Whichever came first.

Plus, she could hardly find joy when embroidering anymore. The darling baby cat stitched on her square looked just as darling and baby-like as everyone else's, but Gloria's artwork left her feeling empty in a way that felt unfamiliar and strange.

"Gloria, dear, did you hear my question?" Ms. Heart asked in that singsong voice that reminded Gloria of wind chimes. Gloria snapped her eyes back to the front of the classroom, where Ms. Heart stood, blinking as her eyes adjusted from the dazzling sunshine outside to the softer light of the classroom. A poster that read *Be the Reason Someone Smiles Today* hung on the wall behind Ms. Heart. Yuck.

"What?" Gloria asked. "I mean . . . I beg your pardon?"

"Gloria, were you zoning out again?"

"I'm so sorry, Ms. Heart," Gloria said, thinking up a good story as an excuse. "I was just watching my friend, um, Domino. He's right outside the window."

Ms. Heart stared at Gloria, puzzled. Turned out Gloria was a quick thinker, a skill that came in handy now that she couldn't keep her mind from wandering.

"Who, dear?" Ms. Heart gazed at Gloria through enormous spectacles that threatened to slide off the tip of her nose. The frames made her eyes look at least five (maybe six) times too large for her head.

"Remember Domino?" How could Ms. Heart possibly remember Domino? Gloria had just come up with the name on the spot. "I simply *must* have told you about Domino!" Gloria put on her most lyrical voice. "He's the cutesy-wootsy little chipmunk that plays on the branch outside." Describing animals in baby talk always worked with Ms. Heart. She couldn't resist a cute animal or, better yet, talking about a cute animal. Ms. Heart's magnified eyes followed where Gloria's outstretched finger pointed. The chipmunk scuttled down the tree trunk and disappeared into a thick patch of yellow tulips. "See?"

Gloria smiled an extra-big smile, showing all her top and bottom teeth.

"Oh, of course. Domino. Okay, dear. Please try to stay with us now."

"Of course, Ms. Heart," Gloria answered. Gloria knew fooling Ms. Heart wasn't very nice. But, as she'd recently discovered, it was *fun*. Thrilling, even. "Will do."

"We were just discussing the merits of Daisy's stitchwork. What do you enjoy most about it?"

Gloria glanced at Daisy, who stood in front of the class next to the kitten photograph Ms. Heart had projected onto the wall. Daisy and her artwork always looked so—how to put it?—organized. Her yellow Sun School uniform was crisp and unstained, her long black hair always brushed and shiny. Daisy's Sun Charm, freshly polished, rested gently in the little dip between her collarbones. The opal-colored charm shimmered when it caught the light, the way Sun Charms always did. In her hand, Daisy held a square of light-blue fabric with a fluffy cat sewn on with light-orange thread. The stitching was even and precise. Frankly, it was flawless.

Then, someone caught Gloria's attention. The small girl who wore her hair in two tight puffs on top of her head, each puff nearly the size of her head, and whose eyes reminded Gloria of outer space, but not in a scary way. That girl.

That girl went by Mitten.

The look on her face . . . her eyes were big, and she leaned forward onto her desk a bit, making her seem extra alert, like she was expecting—no, hoping—for . . . what? Gloria quickly darted her eyes away.

"It's very pretty," Gloria said quickly, and she actually meant it.

"What specifically, Gloria dear?" Ms. Heart batted her eyes in anticipation.

Gloria squinted and thought hard about her next move. She looked down at her square, then back up at Daisy's, then back down to hers, and back at Daisy's. The class waited for her answer patiently.

Gloria could have said the fur on Daisy's kitten was sewn with such accuracy that no thread looked out of place. She could have complimented Daisy on how delicately the kitten's tail curled up over its back. Or she could have praised how

Daisy had managed to create such a stunning piece of art so quickly. Those things were all true. But that's not what stuck out to Gloria about Daisy's artwork.

"It kind of looks like everyone else's," Gloria said finally.

"Thanks!" Daisy chirped.

"I mean . . ." Gloria couldn't help what came out of her mouth next. "It's really good. But you're such a good artist, and I just feel like your square could . . . stand out more."

Let's be honest: Gloria's criticism wasn't small. It was tiny. Minuscule.

Nevertheless, everyone in the classroom collectively gasped. Nobody ever—*ever*—gave negative feedback. Especially for an art project. It simply was not done.

The stunned silence continued. Daisy looked pale. She put her hand on a chair to steady herself. (Daisy tended to faint when she was overwhelmed.)

Gloria again noticed Mitten, whose expression still stood out from the rest. It almost seemed as if Mitten was excited. But Gloria felt bad. Daisy hadn't done anything wrong. Her embroidery was absolutely adequate; it looked just like an orange kitten.

"W-what do you mean?" Daisy asked, her lower lip trembling as she spoke. "What do you mean it could stand out *more*?"

A single tear rolled down Daisy's cheek. Ms. Heart appeared downright confused. Again. For a teacher, she sure was easily confounded.

This wasn't going well. So Gloria took the easy way out.

"What I mean is, why stop with the kitten? I'm sure the people at the nursing home would love to see even more animals, if possible," Gloria suggested. Then, for an extra touch, she added, "Maybe a butterfly?"

That did the trick.

The class erupted into excited chatter, rapidly discussing the best ways to incorporate butterflies into the quilt. Gloria had started the butterfly trend a week ago when Aisha noticed a butterfly Gloria had doodled in her notebook during History of Saints. The next day, every seventh-grade Sun Twin had butterflies drawn on all their notebooks.

Gloria was astonished by the power she seemed to yield. The less she tried, the more popular she became. As far as all the Sun Twins and teachers at Gemini were concerned, Gloria could do no wrong.

"What a wonderful idea, Gloria!" Ms. Heart said, clapping with excitement. But before she could continue, the bell rang, signaling the end of class. (The bell was actually a harp—gentle and delicate, and you really had to listen or you might miss it.) "We'll pick back up with this tomorrow." Everyone stood and began packing up their sewing kits. "Remember, children! We're only a week away from the Gemini Academy Fair next Saturday. We must make haste with our quilt so it is ready on time. Let's make this the best fair yet!"

Gloria's classmates cheered with excitement. Every Sun

Twin just loved the Gemini Academy Fair—the annual event following the Induction Ceremony that welcomed incoming students.

"I can't wait to meet the newbies," Aisha said as she put her sewing materials away.

All the orange thread went in the orange thread box, the blue thread in the blue thread box, the pink thread in the pink thread box, and so on. All boxes were kept on the Sewing Shelf and organized in a line, going from lightest to darkest. Needles were to be returned to the needle jar; scrap thread in the lidded scrap thread bin. Everything had its place in Sun School.

As Gloria cleaned up her workspace, she remembered her first Gemini Academy Fair, seven years ago. The older Sun Twins had planned it that year, too. Everything was exciting, bright, and new. Sun School still felt full of possibility.

"I'm so glad we're planning the fair this year," Aisha remarked. "Last year's was such a bust. It was bad even by Moon School standards."

Aisha wasn't wrong. The responsibility—or *honor*, as Sun Twins would say—to plan and decorate the fair alternated each year. Last year, it had been the Moon Twins' turn and, as a result, the fair had been both chaotic and underwhelming.

"Honestly, we should really just be in charge of the fair aesthetic every year. Remember how awful it was last year?" Aisha complained. Daisy and Lana nodded in agreement, which only encouraged Aisha to continue. "*Improvisation: The Thrill of*

Surprise was the unfriendliest theme ever. Surprises are supposed to be fun, not depressing! All the activity booths were falling apart, the banners were only half-finished, and there wasn't a flower in sight! Totally inconsiderate of them, if you ask me. It's so annoying that we have to even see our Moon Twins at the fair, much less leave it to them to plan it every other year."

Gloria kept quiet. It wasn't worth challenging Aisha when she had her mind made up. Yes, Sun Twins technically *saw* their Moon Twins at the fair, but it wasn't like they had to participate in the same activities or even talk to one another. Most Sun Twins ignored their Moon Twin counterparts entirely.

Most.

"Can you *believe* we used to go to school with our Moon Twins?" Daisy added, shuddering, her face rapidly draining of color once again. "It was only kindergarten, but still."

"Sit down, Daze," Lana said, gently touching her friend's shoulder.

"I don't know why we have to wait until first grade to come to Gemini," Aisha complained. "If I were in charge, we wouldn't have to wait until the Induction Ceremony for our charms." Aisha rubbed the pearly, sun-shaped charm around her neck. "We'd get them at birth."

"Ooh, like birth charms!" Daisy squealed.

"Birth charms. Love it," Aisha said. Daisy always agreed with Aisha, and Aisha always agreed with Daisy. Then, turning to Gloria, Aisha added, "Maybe you should say some-thing about that in your speech at the pep rally. JK, JK. Don't worry; I was only kidding," Aisha reassured, blushing a bit. "Totally a joke."

"Of course," Gloria said. Of course it was a joke. No Sun Class President in their right mind would suggest such an innovation.

"Hey, tell us again that crazy story about your Moon Twin?" Aisha asked excitedly, probably trying to change the subject, in case it was not clear her previous statement was, in fact, a joke.

"Ooh, tell us!" Daisy said, taking a seat in the nearest chair. Daisy was best seated if talk ever turned to their Moon Twins.

"You know, the one from when you were little?" Aisha con-tinued, keeping her voice low.

Talking about your Moon Twin wasn't exactly forbidden, but it wasn't exactly encouraged, either. Most Sun Twins were a little bit afraid of their Moon Twins, even if they wouldn't admit it.

Except for Gloria. Nothing about her Moon Twin, Greta, scared her. This oddity of hers wasn't new; she'd always felt that way, though it was a secret she didn't dare share with even her most trusted friends.

But Gloria couldn't resist an eager audience, so she indulged Aisha's request. "You mean how Greta always used to eat hot dogs when we were younger?" Gloria waited for the shrieks of disgust that were sure to come. In Sun School, eating meat of an unspecified origin was practically a cardinal sin.

"OMG. *So* nasty." Lana giggled with delight. "That's as bad as *my* Moon Twin. She lies and cheats as much as she can."

"How do you know? You haven't talked to your Moon Twin recently, have you?" Aisha asked.

"Of course not! But I'm sure it's true," Lana insisted. "All Moon Twins love to lie and cheat and steal! It's, like, it's written into their DNA."

"They can't be *all* bad," Gloria muttered. It had become increasingly difficult for Gloria to hold her tongue when her friends gossiped about their Moon Twins.

"Oh, come on, Glo, you know they are. Greta especially! Hot dogs are deviant," Aisha said with a truly horrified look on her face.

"Perverse, even," Daisy added, wide-eyed.

Gloria snapped, suddenly enraged. "It's not like *you've* never made a mistake." Gloria could call her Moon Twin whatever name she wanted, but it really made her blood boil when any of her friends did the same.

Daisy and the rest of the girls stared back at Gloria.

"I never have," Daisy said earnestly. "I don't think I've ever made a mistake. Not since I got my Sun Charm, at least."

"Neither have I," Aisha agreed. "Nope, I don't think Daisy or I have ever made a mistake or done anything unkind. Not on purpose, if that's what you mean."

Gloria sighed. She didn't know what she meant anymore. And Daisy and Aisha were probably right. They likely had never intentionally done anything less than kind. They were Sun Twins through and through.

Gloria fiddled with the Sun Charm around her neck, a new habit of hers. Though she'd grown used to wearing the necklace years ago (Gemini Academy students never removed their charm necklaces), she'd started fussing with the charm recently, as if she were suddenly aware of its constant presence around her neck. Ironically, the smooth stone was always a bit cool to the touch. She moved the charm to the back of the chain, concealing it behind her shirt. That was better.

Gloria exited the classroom, followed by Daisy, Aisha, and Lana. They walked down the hallway to their next class, Positivity, Predictability, and Poetry. That week they'd just begun a unit on haiku. Though she kept her opinion to herself, Gloria was not impressed. The form felt rather restrictive, in her humble opinion.

She followed her friends down the hallway, half listening as they discussed the new yellow flower that had just blossomed by the path that led from the Academy building to the Sun Dorms (marigold season was fast approaching), the perfect name for a new puppy (Sunburst), and the virtues of giving back (endless).

Gloria yawned and rubbed her eyes. Nowadays, when she was especially tired, or especially bored, the Sun School aesthetic hurt her eyes. Skylights in every room allowed plenty of sunshine, and shiny wood floors glistened from regular polish. The lockers that lined the hallway were painted a soft pastel yellow. Vivaldi's *The Four Seasons* gently drifted from camouflaged speakers mounted on the ceiling. It was all just a bit too . . . perfect.

As Daisy and Aisha discussed the subjects of their haiku in progress (birthday cake and charity, respectively), Gloria and Lana fell behind.

"Do you want to start fair planning tomorrow at breakfast?" Lana asked. "I'm so excited to really put our Sun stamp on the festivities this year." As Sun Class President, Gloria was required to spearhead the fair planning this year. Lana, Aisha, and Daisy had been anticipating the planning process for weeks, eager to assist Gloria with all the preplanning, planning, and setup for Gemini Fair. Which was great, as far as Gloria was concerned. She'd been doing a lot of reflection these past two months, two weeks, and two days, and she'd realized something about herself: She now considered herself an idea girl. An idea girl, but not so much of a "plan and execute in an organized fashion" kind of girl.

"You bet," Gloria replied.

"I can't wait to find out the theme this year!" Lana clapped her hands together and hopped in the air. "I love setting up and decorating the Gemini Academy Fair almost as much as I love the fair itself!"

Just then, Gloria spotted Mitten. She had to move her legs twice as fast, it seemed, to keep up with the other Sun Twins. Still, she was falling behind.

"Hey, Mitten," Lana said as they came up behind her.

Mitten peered up at them, wide-eyed, for a moment before responding. "Hi."

Gloria remembered the way Mitten had looked at her during class.

"Oh, your backpack is open," Lana cautioned.

"Shoot, I always do that. Thanks," Mitten said, clumsily struggling with her backpack.

That's when Gloria saw it, poking out of Mitten's bag. And once she saw it, she didn't want to peel her eyes away.

"Is that your embroidery patch?" Gloria asked.

Mitten looked down and blushed. "Oh, yeah."

"What's it doing in your backpack?" Lana asked suspiciously. "I don't think you're supposed to take it out of the class—"

"Ms. Heart said it was okay," Mitten answered quickly.

"Phew," Lana said with an exhale. "I thought for a second you were breaking a rule!"

"Oh, no. I wanted to take it back to the dorms to work on it some more tonight." Mitten shyly tucked the fabric back into her bag.

"Wait," Gloria interjected. "Can I see?"

Mitten looked at Lana, then back at Gloria. Hesitantly,

Mitten pulled the embroidery patch out of her pack and held it in her hands.

Stitched on to the fabric was a pale orange kitten. Two ears, four legs, and a tail. Just like everybody else's. But also not. Something about the way the kitten looked—like it was mid-breath, mid-stretch, or even mid-purr. Gloria wasn't sure. It felt . . . *alive*, somehow. She could see it chasing after a ball of yarn. She could imagine the soft texture of its fur. She didn't need a butterfly or anything else on the swatch to make it great. Mitten's kitten packed a punch all on its own.

"Wow," Gloria whispered. "I *love* it. How did you . . ." Gloria's voice trailed off.

"It's really cute," Lana added.

"Thanks!" Mitten smiled. "I really like art class."

"I know—it reminds me of Domino," Gloria blurted, satisfied she could put a finger on it.

"Domino is a chipmunk, silly. How could Mitten's kitten look like Domino?" Lana teased.

"Never mind." Gloria was suddenly very confused as to why she'd said that. It wasn't worth explaining.

"Okay. See ya." Mitten tucked the swatch back into her bag and scuttled ahead.

"Okeydokey," Lana chirped.

Once Mitten was out of earshot, Lana said, "She's . . . I don't know what she is."

"I like her," Gloria said, still in a daze.

"Of course. That's what I meant. Of course, I like her, too," Lana agreed.

But that's not what Gloria was thinking. Gloria was thinking about Mitten's artwork. Something about it made her want to keep the image in her mind forever.

And it seemed that Gloria might. She thought about Mitten's picture all during poetry class. While she was supposed to be working on her haiku about a soft summer breeze, Gloria thought about how Mitten's swatch was somehow different from everybody else's, and even though she couldn't articulate it, the fact that it was different at all excited her. Daisy's patch would be better if it looked more like Mitten's. But why had Mitten's reminded her of Domino for that split second? How was hers different from the rest? It was the same orange cat, posing the same way. She used the same thread as the rest of the class. Why could Gloria imagine Mitten's cat purring? Why did it seem to somehow exist in real life? What could it be?

It wasn't until she walked into the dining hall for the pep rally that it hit her. She still didn't know *how* Mitten had done it, but Gloria realized what made Mitten's picture impossible to forget.

It was her favorite.

The Sun School dining hall had high, arched ceilings accented by wooden beams and white stone floors. In it stood four rows of sturdy wooden tables along which Sun Twins sat in simple white chairs. At dinnertime, the setting sun filtered through the large windows, giving the entire room a warm, comforting glow. It was a bright, grand space.

Gloria sat in her usual seat next to Lana, across from Aisha and Daisy. Gloria drummed her fingers on the table, impatiently waiting for Headmistress Solis to get the show on the road.

The Sun Class President always gave a speech at the pep rally preceding the Gemini Academy Fair. It was Gloria's responsibility to help get her fellow Sun Twins excited for the upcoming event, relay that year's theme, and outline the lineup of festivities.

Gloria was ready to take the stage; she loved giving speeches. The thrill of being in front of everyone, onstage, in the spotlight, made her tingle from head to toe. Of course, her remarks were carefully planned and memorized, but being in front of a crowd, well, anything could happen. That possibility both scared and thrilled Gloria.

In fact, Gloria was more excited for her speech about Gemini Academy Fair than she was for the fair itself. She didn't like that fact, but there was no denying the truth. Yup, Gloria just wasn't all that pumped about Gemini Academy Fair this year. She knew exactly what was coming, for it was the same every year Sun School was in charge. The same was pleasant (there was always comfort to be found in the familiar), and certainly better than any Moon School–planned event, but not exactly something worth looking forward to at this point.

But her speech was. At least the adrenaline of speaking in front of her fellow Sun Twins got her heart thumping.

Finally, Headmistress Solis stood and approached the small podium at the front of the hall.

"Good evening, dear Sun Twins," she said into the microphone. Her voice was soft and light, like a pillow.

"Good evening, Headmistress Solis," everyone chimed in unison.

Headmistress Solis very much interested Gloria. Perhaps it was because the Headmistress was—well, how to put it?— fascinating. That was mainly due to her appearance. Headmistress Solis was very old. She'd been the principal of Sun School since basically forever. Despite her age (which nobody seemed to know for sure), she was still very glamorous, at least in Gloria's opinion. She always wore a canary-yellow head wrap with two tendrils of silver hair dangling from above her temples. One of her eyes was bright blue and the other was hazel; *heterochromatic*, she called it, *nothing to be afraid of*. Gloria had never seen her without a cup of tea in her hand, and she always smelled like peanut butter. Gloria did not like peanut butter one bit, but she still felt a fondness toward Headmistress Solis, despite her scent.

"Another Gemini Academy Fair fast approaches," she began with a smile. "Before I let Miss Garcia get to the details, just a few reminders about logistics and safety."

Headmistress Solis gave a rundown of how the fair was to work. Yawn. Everyone present had heard this speech before, but they listened patiently all the same. The Gemini Academy Fair was the only time of year when Sun Twins and Moon Twins were allowed to interact with one another, and it always caused problems.

"Be warned." Headmistress Solis's cheerful voice became suddenly grave. "If any Moon Twins try to lure you into any of their activities or to enlist you in any aggressive or rowdy behavior during the fair, do remember to disengage and stay calm."

Every Sun Twin nodded as worried looks swept over the student body.

But just as things seemed to get a little too bleak for Sun School, Headmistress Solis smiled and held her arms out wide, as if to invite everyone in for a gigantic hug. "Lastly, remember that this is an occasion to celebrate, an opportunity to welcome new Sun Twins into our community, and a time to champion the virtues that help define Sun School: support, teamwork, and, of course, love."

Gloria was eager for Headmistress Solis to finish her remarks. As much as the actual fair was celebratory and fun, the Induction Ceremony that preceded the festivities marked the saddest day of Gloria's life: the day she was separated from her sister, her twin.

Greta.

Gloria pushed the thought out of her head and resisted a sudden urge to play with the food in front of her. Tonight's dinner was broccoli soup and croutons, with a small dish of blackberries, a smaller dish of raspberries, and a tiny plate topped with one single strawberry. Sun meals were always nutritious, organic, and served on separate plates so no two foods ever touched.

"Now, without further ado, please welcome your Sun Class President, Gloria Garcia!"

The Sun Twins cheered as Gloria rose and walked to the podium. Headmistress Solis received Gloria with her signature embrace, a hug so genuine and hearty, Gloria felt as if she were in a cocoon. *A cocoon with peanut butter walls*, Gloria thought, holding her breath.

Gloria turned toward the podium. She looked at the four long dining tables along which her fellow Sun Twins sat quietly, napkins on their laps, with perfect posture. Suddenly, she felt very small.

So she took a breath. A big one. That was better. A buzz of excitement fluttered through her chest. She began.

"When I say *Gemini*, you say *Fair*! GEMINI!"

"FAIR!" the Sun Twins chanted back, enthusiastically. Obediently.

"GEMINI!"

"FAIR!"

"When I say *mari*, you say *gold*! MARI!"

"GOLD!"

"MARI!"

"GOLD!"

Gloria smiled.

"When I say *sharing*, you say *caring*! SHARING!"

"CARING!"

"SHARING!"

"CARING!"

The Sun School student body chanted along with gusto.

"And that, my fellow Sun Twins, is the theme of this year's Gemini Academy Fair!" More cheers and applause erupted throughout the dining hall. "As Headmistress Solis mentioned, all your favorite activities will be back, as sunny as always!"

The energy Gloria received from the audience gave her confidence. She was feeling better, more herself. Gloria glanced down at her note cards and squinted. Gloria was getting excited; she wanted to read from her notes just in case.

"As you know, everything will take place on the Great Lawn. There will be some spots dedicated for Moon activities, but don't worry—everything will still appear as organized and sunny as ever! We'll have a trust-fall station in the north tent and an ongoing basketball game on the south court. Next to the refreshment tables on the east side of the fairgrounds, we'll have a flower-arranging station, and on the west side, of course, there will be the famous Sun School cookie bar! Sun-shaped lemon butter cookies for all!"

The dining hall exploded with cheer and merriment (well, far more than usual, anyway). Gloria knew the cookie bar would get them excited just as it had two years ago, and the two years before that, and the two years before that. Decadent and sugary treats were few and far between in Sun School. *Lemon butter cookies never fail*, she thought.

"And last but not least," she added, "don't forget to check out the kitten quilt made by the members of Ms. Heart's Inspirational Art class, which will be donated to the Geminus County Nursing Home after the fair."

At that moment, an image of Mitten's and Daisy's embroidery patches popped into her head.

Gloria had an idea. A great idea. A great idea that made her so excited she blurted it out without thinking it through. It was just too great to keep to herself.

"And I just thought of a way to make this year's Gemini Academy Fair better than ever before!" A rush of excited whispers flurried through the dining hall. "We all love art projects, right?" Gloria pressed on, not waiting for a response. "Next to the kitten quilt, we can have a mural wall!"

The idea sounded even better now that she'd said it aloud. A mural wall—genius! What better way to celebrate community and cooperation than a collaborative art project! "We can all add to it throughout the day. Then, at the end, we'll have something created by everyone that will bring us into the year ahead. What do you all think?"

A silence that was somehow louder than anything Gloria had ever heard overtook the dining space. Somewhere in the back of the room a fork clattered on the floor. The metallic sound echoed through the hall. Gloria paused and regarded her peers. Dozens of girls in clean yellow blouses tucked into matching yellow shorts gazed back at her.

A hand popped up in the very back of the grand room. It was Mitten.

"Yes, Mitten, do you have a question?"

Everyone in the dining hall swiveled their heads to look at Mitten, the silence overruled by the noise of students adjusting in their wooden seats. She stood up and held her hands behind her back. Gloria had the impression that those hands of hers were fidgeting back there. "Where will we paint the mural? Like, on an actual wall?"

All eyes turned back to Gloria. Even Headmistress Solis gazed upon her, mouth open in anticipation. Or horror. Or both.

Gloria's mind raced. She hadn't thought about the fact that a mural wall actually required a *wall*. "We'll . . . we'll paint on the same material we use for the booth banners. There's always extra. Let's put it to good use!"

It felt as if all the positivity had been sucked out of the room. What sounded like three more utensils crashed to the ground. Daisy fainted; Aisha caught her by the ponytail a moment before she face-planted into her broccoli soup.

Aisha raised her free hand. Gloria pointed a trembling finger her way—she was suddenly too afraid to speak. She wasn't sure she could trust the words that might come out of her own mouth.

"Are you . . . are you implying that Gemini Academy Fair isn't good enough the way it is?"

Gloria's mind was doing overtime now, working quickly to find a good answer to Aisha's question. "I didn't mean—"

Silence.

Gloria tried again. "I just thought that—"

Silence.

"I meant . . . as an *additional* way to give back. You know, um . . . sharing the creation of art."

More silence.

"I just thought . . ." Gloria locked eyes with Lana, who stared back at Gloria, eyes wide, and shrugged her shoulders. "I don't know what I thought."

Gloria gave up. For the first time ever, she hadn't been able to talk herself out of a problem. She didn't realize suggesting something new would be so complicated.

But it was too late. The floodgates were open. Hands burst

up around the dining hall like fish in an aquarium popping to the surface to retrieve food, but nobody waited to be called on. The Sun School dining hall devolved into disorganized chatter, Sun Twins shouting their opinions at will, no one waiting for their turn to speak.

"I don't like change!"

"Will our horrid Moon Twins be involved?!"

"What if this accidentally promotes competition?!"

"What if a Moon Twin paints something mean on the mural?!"

"Will we even have enough paint?!"

"Do we even have a permit for this?!"

Absolute chaos. Daisy had full-on fainted into her soup this time. Voices and shouts mixed together like a broken symphony. In a last-ditch effort to restore order, Gloria cried, "I just thought doing something different this year might be fun!"

But it was no use. Gloria sighed and dropped her head, ashamed.

Headmistress Solis came from behind Gloria and clapped her hands twice. The sharp sound pierced through the dining hall and the Sun Twins fell silent. "Miss Garcia, we appreciate your suggestion, but it sounds like you may have misspoken. You know as well as any Sun Twin that the Gemini Academy Fair is about tradition. It's wonderful just the way it is, and there is no need to confuse things by adding an additional art project when we already have other lovely options."

"I know, I'm sorry. I didn't mean to imply . . . it's just that—" Gloria looked up at Headmistress Solis. The principal nodded, as if urging Gloria to continue her apology. "I must have woken up on the Moon side of the bed this morning." The dining hall released a collective—yet nervous—laugh.

Gloria felt something that was totally unfamiliar: She'd failed. Completely and utterly failed. Nope, Gloria did not feel like herself, not one bit.

Gloria ripped her note cards in two, shoved the torn pieces deep into her pocket, and trudged offstage. As she made the long and lonely walk to the doors at the opposite end of the hall, the eyes of her fellow students following her progression, she wished she could simply disappear.

Gloria went straight to Sun Dorm and kept to herself for the rest of the night. She quickly brushed her teeth, changed into pajamas, and tucked herself into bed. Gloria was the first to bed, but she was the last to fall asleep. The humiliation she felt from the pep rally continued to sink its claws deeper into her skin. Gloria pulled her knees tighter to her chest and stared out the window. Though it was only barely dusk, she saw the faint outline of a full moon emerge low in the sky. She was surprised how bright the moon shined as the sky continued to darken. *A full moon isn't that different from a sun,* Gloria thought as sleep began to take over. *Or a star.*

● ● ●

As Gloria and the Sun Twins slept, the very last remnants of the day faded into the night. A dense fog rolled in, and soon behind it, thick clouds, teeming with precipitation. Chipmunks retreated deeper into their burrows, butterflies took shelter beneath fallen leaves deep in the nearby woods, and flowers wilted and became stringy weeds. The polished marble walls of Gemini Academy buildings faded to a cold gray stone; inky black vines crawled up the turrets toward the slate roof. Lightning flashed; the transformation was nearly complete. As sheets of rain poured down from the thunderous sky, the enormous crest above the double-doored entryway to the main castle faded from a radiant, shining sun to a glistening crescent moon.

Sun School was over.

Time for Moon School to begin.

CHAPTER TWO
GRETA

Greta Garcia stood outside the three-point line, dribbling the ball back and forth.

Right, left, right, left.

She focused her eyes on the basket. The Moon School gym was hazy. The already-dim lights flickered. Each bounce of the ball kicked up a cloud of dust. Greta's nose tingled, but she refused to let herself be distracted by something as ridiculous as an oncoming sneeze.

Greta was determined to score—determined to prove that she belonged on the court, that she had what it took to make it onto the first team. The first team of the seventh BLASTketball squad, of course. The Gemini Academy Fair, when the biggest annual BLASTketball exhibition match was held, was only one week away. It was now or never. Only one Moon Twin stood in her way.

Lola.

Greta glanced at the giant shot clock on the wall. Twenty seconds until the BLASTketball detonated. Plenty of time.

"Let's see what you got," Lola taunted as Greta approached. Lola's brown eyes narrowed and her chaotic topknot haloed around her like an unruly mane.

Greta swallowed. She wouldn't let herself be intimidated. Not this time.

It's simple, just follow the play and you'll be fine, she reminded herself. She kicked back her feet to make sure her knee pads were secured.

"Dashes to Ashes!" she yelled. *"Dashes to Ashes!"* Her mouth guard made the words come out sloppy and jumbled.

Everyone jumped into action. Tashi and Rox made diagonal runs across the paint and tackled the forwards who guarded under the basket. Mara pulled Sierra by one of her many short braids, throwing her off-kilter. The play was unfolding perfectly.

Time for Greta to make her move—her big move that would get her past Lola and enable her to score: trip Lola, then drive to the basket.

Greta considered how to execute. She might be able to get Lola if she stuck out her right leg, but that would require her to dribble with her left hand.

Lola neared.

Or if Greta got closer, maybe a hip check would serve the same purpose as a leg trip. That seemed like another reasonable option. A hip trip.

Yeah, she'd go with the hip trip. Greta crossed the ball to her right hand and dribbled forward when a better option presented itself.

Greta saw an opening—just a slot, really—amid the madness that provided a narrow, unobstructed lane to the basket. She would have to sneak through quickly, but that wouldn't be a problem. Greta had experience sneaking.

Greta crossed the ball to her left hand and accelerated forward, past Lola, past Tashi, Mara, and the rest of them. She took one last dribble, then a giant step with her right foot. Now under the basket, Greta lifted the ball to her chest to shoot an easy layup when—

SLAM!

Greta was tackled from behind by a force that felt larger than life. A tidal wave? A bear? A flesh-eating monster?

Nope.

Lola. It had to be Lola.

Greta flew forward, out of control. The ball slipped from her grasp as she crashed to the ground, first her hands, then elbows (protected with pads, luckily), and then knees (protected with more pads). Her head thundered down, followed by the pearly, crescent-shaped Moon Charm that hung from a simple chain around her neck. It made a tinny sound as it hit the floor.

A shrill whistle pierced Greta's eardrums.

"No, no, no!" Coach Sliver yelled from the sideline. She blew her whistle again, signaling for the shot clock to pause. "What was that?!"

Everyone groaned. They knew what was coming. So did Greta.

Greta lay still on the crusty gym floor. She clenched her eyelids shut and willed herself to disappear.

No luck.

"Lola—great hit. Nice and late. Excellent defense—that's how you stop her! I love the creativity you bring to the court. A full-body bear tackle from behind—genius." Coach Sliver's voice suddenly took a sinister turn. "But Greta—that was terrible! Garbage! Downright despicable!" Coach Sliver screamed, throwing her clipboard on the ground.

Greta sighed. Despite her best efforts, she had yet to disappear.

Coach Sliver's heavy footsteps approached. Reluctantly, Greta pushed up to her knees and turned to face her.

Coach Sliver wore black steel-toe boots and an eye patch. *Dress the part*, Coach Sliver sometimes muttered under her breath when she was in a particularly foul mood. Greta didn't know if the patch was for fashion or for function. Either way, it was both confusing and creepy. She kept the stringy gray hair on the right side of her scalp long, and the left side of her head shaved, revealing a large pink birthmark in the shape of a star. She had the biggest and the yellowest teeth Greta had ever seen, and her breath smelled faintly of peanut butter— which Greta *hated*. Yup, Coach Sliver fit right into Moon School, no doubt about it.

Coach Sliver was also the Moon School principal. *I'm a natural born enforcer,* she liked to brag. Long before she coached BLASTketball, she still went by *Coach* Sliver.

"We've been practicing Dashes to Ashes all *week*! If you don't trip the defender *before* you drive to the basket, you won't score. It's as simple as that!" Coach Sliver fumed. "If you don't adopt this strategy, you're never going to succeed at this sport."

"I just thought—"

"You thought what? That you could win using your speed and ball skills alone?"

Greta nodded. She heard Lola snicker. Greta stared at the dusty floor.

"This is *BLAST*ketball, Greta. *Not* basketball!"

"Boo, basketball," said Lola under her breath.

Greta nodded. She felt ashamed, embarrassed, and alone.

Greta desperately needed to find her *thing.* That was what had gotten her into this whole BLASTketball debacle in the first place. She had the dexterity for fireball archery, but the flames got too hot for her delicate hands to bear. She had the power for dagger throwing, but not the accuracy (which was essential). And after several practices, Greta came to the obvious conclusion that hurdle jumping wasn't for her, either; jumping over trenches teeming with lizards caused her eyes to water uncontrollably (Greta was hyperallergic to reptile dandruff).

That left BLASTketball. Which at first seemed like it could be the perfect fit (and safe; protective padding was required).

Greta was naturally spry and liked to sprint short distances. Plus, some of the wildest, baddest, and altogether most wicked Moon Twins played BLASTketball. *Maybe, just maybe,* Greta thought, *I could be one of them, too.*

Yup, Greta was certain that if she could make a statement on the BLASTketball court, her life off the court could also greatly improve. She was the type to eat lunch alone, and she was an easy target for anything from airborne burritos to insults. It was getting old.

But BLASTketball was starting to become an absolutely soul-crushing pursuit. It was becoming harder and harder to ignore that maybe, just maybe, this sport was not Greta's thing, either. But if not BLASTketball, then what?

She didn't want to think about it. It was too depressing. So Greta plodded to the far end of the court to retrieve the ball as Coach Sliver continued to rant.

"This may be a team sport, but you are not to engage in any team*work.* Teamwork does not win games, and most certainly does not win championships. Do you hear me, Greta? Is that clear?"

Greta nodded.

"Teamwork and foul play do not—I repeat, do *not*—go hand in hand. Do you understand me?"

Greta nodded. Coach Sliver liked the sound of her own voice.

"Foul play is the pillar of this game! It is the only way to score, the only way to win. You cannot succeed without mastering the fine and delicate art of foul play—in sports *and* in life!" Coach Sliver was pacing now. She tended to pace when she ranted.

Greta couldn't put a finger on it, but something about foul play felt—how to put it?—rude? Sure. Inefficient? Unnecessary? Maybe. But that wasn't quite it.

Greta sighed. No, it wasn't foul play that was the problem. It was her. She just had to try harder: trip more sneakily, ponytail-pull with more vigor, shove with real commitment.

"Let's review one last time," Coach Sliver commanded. "What is the founding principle of foul play?"

"To inflict damage!" Mara yelled excitedly. Greta had known Mara since first grade, the very beginning of her time at Gemini Academy. She didn't trust the shifty brunette then and didn't trust her now. Greta suspected it had to do with her bangs. Something about the way Mara brushed them into points reminded her of shark teeth. Or fangs. Or both.

"Close, Mara."

"It's *Chopper*. I go by Chopper now," Mara insisted. Coach Sliver ignored her.

"Inflicting damage is a side effect. And a delightful one at that," Coach Sliver corrected. "We use foul play because that is the best way to win. Name for me three principal foul-play tactics," Coach Sliver thundered. Yup, Coach Sliver loved the sound of her own voice. Especially when her own voice was very, very loud.

"Trip from behind!" Lola offered, without missing a beat.

"Elbow to the ribs!" Rox screamed.

"Hair-pulling!" Sierra squeaked, rubbing the root of one of her braids.

"Three excellent, classic examples. Very, very good," Coach Sliver said. "But remember: You are not limited to those options. Be aggressive! Be unpredictable! Invent your own rules!"

Greta gulped. This was exactly why foul play was so confusing for her. The rules always seemed to change!

"If you keep the moves dirty," Coach Sliver began, licking her lips as though she were about to sink her teeth into a juicy double cheeseburger, "*nothing* can stop you."

Dirty! That's it! Greta had an idea. She'd use a kind of foul play that had never been covered before—one of her own invention.

"Don't forget about dirty looks!" Greta shouted. She was eager to participate. Eager to show Coach Sliver that she knew her stuff. The blundered trip in the last play was a mistake, a fluke. Nothing more. "Dirty looks are the best!"

Silence. Coach Sliver stared at her but didn't respond.

Three seconds passed. Sierra played with a small pet snake she'd produced from her pocket (she always had that small reptile on her person). Chopper glared at Greta, mouthing something Greta couldn't make out.

Greta was getting nervous. "You know, because a dirty look, if it's a really filthy, truly scary face, can really intimidate a defender. And then, if they're intimidated, it will be easy to get past them, right?"

More silence. Rox spun a greasy strand of black hair around her finger. Tashi chewed on her mouth guard. Lola sighed (or was it a growl?) and rolled her eyes.

For the second time that practice, Greta willed herself to disappear.

And for the second time, no luck.

Coach Sliver took two deliberate and truly terror-inducing steps toward Greta, who had never been this close to Coach Sliver's face before. She noticed the coach's eye patch was dirty and sweat collected on her upper lip.

"The fact that you are still incapable of grasping the basics of this incredibly intuitive sport . . ." Spittle flew from Coach Sliver's mouth and landed on Greta's forehead. Her breath smelled like she brushed it with peanut-butter toothpaste. "I'm very disappointed in you. I thought you might have had what it takes."

Greta gripped her Moon Charm tightly in her fist. The edges of the crescent threatened to break through her skin and draw blood.

"Oh, give her a break, Coach Sliver," Lola said sweetly. Too sweetly. "She can't help it; she's just so *nice*."

"Ooh, burn," Rox said, loud enough for anyone in outer space to hear. "Good one, Lola." Rox held out her hand for Lola to high-five, but Lola ignored her. Instead, she stood still, feet planted, and stared straight at Greta.

Greta felt all the blood in her body rush to her cheeks. The court went silent once again.

"What did you say?" Greta peeped. She was trembling now, out of anger. Or maybe something else.

Lola took a step toward her. The girls stood head-to-head.

"You heard me," Lola sneered. "Look at you, with your shirt tucked in and your hair all neat. You're such a goody-goody, not messy, nice girl—you may as well be a *Sun Twin*."

Everyone on the BLASTketball court gasped. That was a low blow. Of all things Lola could have said, that was the worst, the meanest, the most horrific. *Sun Twin?* Greta had been called a lot of things. But never *Sun Twin*. That was a phrase rarely uttered during Moon School hours.

Yup, Greta officially hated Lola.

Greta quickly untucked her shirt and rustled her hair, but before Greta could think of a comeback, Coach Sliver blew her whistle.

"Excellent trash-talking," Coach Sliver praised. "Very, very advanced." A sly smile appeared on her face that made Greta's stomach flip, as if it were crawling with worms. "Now let's get on with it. The BLASTketball is live; the blast switch is back on. Keep your eyes on the clock because I will *not* be bailing you out. Ball's in play!" Coach Sliver blew her whistle, and the shot clock started counting down again.

Everyone ran into position while Greta dribbled the ball up the court, taking her time. She took a deep breath and listened to the hollow sound the BLASTketball made with every bounce.

Focus, she thought.

Greta gulped once, then gulped again. But she kept dribbling. She had Lola to beat and a basket to score.

"Think outside the box if you have to!" Coach Sliver commanded from the sideline. "I'm ready to be impressed. Show me something I've never seen before!" Greta kept her eyes focused downcourt. She wouldn't let Coach Sliver's threats intimidate her. She couldn't. "I'm looking at *you*, Garcia."

As Greta dribbled to the top of the key, she sunk in to her knees. Lower to the ground now, each dribble became shorter and quicker. Right-Left. Right-Left. Greta took a deep breath as Lola approached to defend.

Coach Sliver's instructions spun through her brain. *Think outside the box*. Was a jump shot considered inside or outside the box? It wasn't foul play, but maybe, just maybe, it would go in, and she'd score, and that would be all that mattered.

Nope. Greta was definitely too far away to shoot. She'd have to get closer no matter what.

Who cares if it's an airball? Greta rationalized. *That's better than a failed trip, a too-light shove, an elbow in the air instead of the gut!*

"C'mon, *Sun Twin*, bring it," Lola taunted under her breath.

Greta furrowed her brow and clenched her teeth. Sweat trickled down her backbone. No, she wasn't going to take a jump shot. No way. Instead, Greta waited.

Let Lola come to you, she thought.

And that's exactly what Lola did.

Lola charged toward Greta, just as she had the play before, but this time Greta ducked away to the left. Lola almost skidded past her, catching herself just in time.

"Think you're some hotshot now?"

Greta refused to take the bait.

Instead, she faked to the right. Lola nearly fell for it. But she didn't. And now Greta was stuck, unable to pass, unable to dribble.

You're still okay, Greta thought, trying not to panic. *You got this. Let Lola come to you.*

And again, that's exactly what Lola did.

Lola lunged toward Greta, both hands out. At the last second, right before Lola's outstretched arms reached her torso, Greta stuck out her foot, fabulously entangling her leg in Lola's.

Lola went flying. Greta found the splat Lola made when she landed in a belly flop on the floor to be extremely satisfying.

To seal the deal, Greta gave Lola the dirtiest look she could muster.

Ha! Greta thought. *That will show her. That will show everyone!*

Suddenly, a thundering buzzer rumbled through the gym.

The shot clock! Greta had been so focused on tripping Lola that she had forgotten about the shot clock!

She stared down at the BLASTketball—still in her hands—in horror.

The ball came alive. It hiccupped. It burped. It trembled. And then—the blast!

Hisss.

The ball released a silent but deadly-smelling gas that circulated through the gym in mere seconds.

The smell of flowers and freshly mown grass filled the air.

Everyone on the court groaned in horror. Sierra gave her snake emergency CPR. Chopper nervously stroked her pointiest bang with one hand and covered her nose with the other.

"You're so nasty!" Lola sneered.

"*So* nasty," Rox echoed.

Luckily for Greta and everyone else, at that moment the bell (the sound of a bloodcurdling scream) sounded. Practice was over.

As Greta shuffled out of the gym, she felt an ice-cold hand grasp her shoulder. She turned to find herself face-to-face with Coach Sliver, who stared down at Greta with a single, hazel eye.

"Poor effort," Coach Sliver said, shaking her head. "Not first-team material at all."

A terrible, truly nauseating thought occurred to Greta. What if she *had* found her thing? What if it was what Lola said? What if Greta's *thing* was that she was a Sun Twin?

For a Moon Twin, nothing could be worse than that.

Most Moon Meals opened with a Moon Chant. Not that it was enforced. But why not start off a meal screaming and banging fists? From an empty table in the far corner of the dining hall, Greta just listened while her classmates chanted. Greta wasn't feeling all that chant-y today. She mouthed the words, but no sound came out. After the dreadful BLASTketball practice, Greta just wasn't in the mood to participate.

Kick, push, trip, bite
Moon Twins, Moon Twins
Fight, fight, fight!

The chant ended, and everyone dug into their dinner. Greta absently poked the food in front of her with her index finger. Eating with utensils was discouraged at Moon School; Greta didn't even know where to begin looking for a fork. Greta preferred Taco Tuesday to Fried Food Friday. Today it was chicken-fried corn dogs with a side of fried macaroni. No vegetables (Greta loved vegetables) in sight. But that didn't matter. Greta wasn't hungry.

The Moon School mess hall was dark and shadowy, designed to keep Moon Twins guessing about what might be lurking in the corners, Greta suspected. The walls were made of damp stone, and the ceilings were unnecessarily high. She didn't have to look up to know that hundreds of bats hung from the rafters, their beady red eyes staring at the Moon Twins below. Those bats always made Greta feel like she was being hunted. Nope, Greta was not the biggest fan of bats.

Moon School mealtimes were stressful for Greta. That was when Greta always felt the loneliest.

Greta watched Lola's table from across the dining hall. Lola's crew consisted of Rox Rodriguez, a tall, skinny girl with oversize red-framed glasses who wanted to be just like Lola (it was so obvious); Mara "Chopper" Malihi, the one with the terrifying bangs who also liked to pretend her long, thick braid was a helicopter blade; and tiny Sierra Shaw, the reptile lover who talked only to her pet snake if she could help it. Tashi Tak sat at the edge of the table reading a comic book and sucking on a neon lollipop. Her lips and tongue were stained a radioactive blue. And then there was, of course, Lola Lewis, the meanest, bossiest, and messiest Moon Twin in Gemini Academy history. Lola sat on the table tossing individual macaronis into her mouth. Rox and Chopper tried to stab each other in the eye with empty corn dog sticks. Sierra sat under the table feeding pieces of macaroni that missed Lola's mouth to her snake. It was unclear if Lola, Rox, or Tashi knew that Sierra was even there. Occasionally, Lola made a comment Greta couldn't make out and they all laughed. No, Moon Twins didn't laugh; they cackled.

None of those girls liked Greta, but that was fine. Greta wasn't their biggest fan, either. Not one bit.

Greta let her eyes drift away from the popular Moon Twins, who she didn't like at all.

The floor in the Moon School mess hall made Greta dizzy. It was composed of irregularly shaped tiles of all different colors, shapes, and sizes. Well, all common Moon School colors, common Moon School colors being mud brown, blood red, bruise purple, and a silver so bright that if you looked at it too long your eyeballs hurt. She suspected that was the point.

A poster advertising a Moon Twin activity at the upcoming Gemini Academy Fair hung crookedly on the wall by Greta's seat. *Don't miss the luxurious Trash-Talking Lounge! Cool off with a cup of Moon Punch while talking your best smack!*

They were all over Moon School, each one advertising a different attraction:

You bring the insects; we got the deep fryer!

Trophies for the best-of-the-best! Try your Moon hand at fireball archery, dagger throwing, and the gator walk!

Forget sharing; try scaring!

Greta had noticed Coach Sliver haphazardly slapping the posters up over the past couple of weeks. Sun Twins were organizing the fair this year, and Moon Twins had been grumbling about it for a while now. Though she'd never admit it, Greta didn't mind the years that Sun Twins were in charge of the fair. Sure, the themes Sun School thought up were just plain bizarre (*Trust or Bust* seemed like a suspiciously optimistic doctrine to go by), and the all-yellow decorations were a bit trying on the eyes, but at least everything was completed and organized. And, secretly, Greta really appreciated the participation stickers they received after doing *anything*.

When Moon Twins planned the fair, everything was done at the very last minute, if at all, and the decorations lacked any spunk. This year, Greta was certain all the booths would be built, functional, and correctly advertised (there was big drama last year when the sword-swallowing workshop was mismarked as a poetry reading).

Though the Moon activities always varied, the poster advertising the awards ceremony remained the same year after year: It showed a picture of the legendary BLASTketball star Kimora "Knuckles" Kruger holding a giant trophy over her head. A crowd of Moon Twins cheered in the background. Kimora looked proud, tough, and happy.

Greta wanted to be that girl.

Sun Twin. How dare she? thought Greta. She couldn't get the phrase out of her head. *Sun Twin*. Sucking at foul play didn't make her a Sun Twin! She loved jumping on beds and trading insults (well, she didn't *love* that part), and she enjoyed general havoc just like the rest of her peers. She was as much a Moon Twin as the rest of them. Just because she didn't excel at foul play, that made her a Sun Twin? Nonsense. Right?

Greta swatted a moth away from her face and gazed out the window. Rain pelted against the brittle glass. Thunder grumbled. Just another average stormy evening at Gemini Academy. Average for Moon School hours, that is.

Rumor had it that during Sun School—daytime—the mess hall looked totally different. The entire school did. She had only heard what sounded like fantastical descriptions from her *actual* Sun Twin sister, Gloria, during one of their secret weekly meet-ups. Soft-yellow lockers? Blue skies and sunshine? Blossoming flower gardens, orderly classrooms, and posters emphasizing the value of positive reinforcement? If Greta didn't know better, she'd think Gloria was making it all up.

But Gloria wouldn't do that. Gloria and Greta always told each other the truth.

Speaking of Gloria, it was almost time. In just a few hours, when the dark faded into dawn, when it wasn't totally night but not yet morning, it would be time to meet her sister.

Every Saturday morning, Greta snuck out just after bedtime, an hour before sunrise, and Gloria slipped away an hour before the morning alarm sounded. Gloria and Greta named this special hour—the brief time that was either late Friday night or early Saturday morning, depending how you looked at it—Fraturday. The sisters met, under the cover of twilight, at the edge of Lake Vetiti. Sometimes they did the last of their most-procrastinated homework side by side (often ethics for Gloria and Poison Arts for Greta), sometimes they complained about the week past, and sometimes they just took a swim, floating on the surface of the water in silence, hand in hand, gazing at the dark, cloudy sky.

Greta liked those days the best.

Nobody knew about Fraturday other than Greta and Gloria. Not just because Lake Vetiti was outside Gemini Academy grounds and therefore visiting was forbidden, and not only because no other Moon Twin wanted anything to do with their Sun Twin (at least as far as either of the Garcia sisters knew). Nope. Greta and Gloria were the only students at Gemini Academy who knew about Fraturday because they had made it up. It was their invention—their secret.

Fraturday belonged to Greta and Gloria alone, and they intended to keep it that way.

The pitch-black sky was starting to lighten in the distance. It was almost daybreak; almost time for bed. Greta took a first and last bite of her chicken-fried corn dog, picked up her plate, and stood to go.

Suddenly, something squishy, wet, and completely putrid smashed into Greta's forehead. Sour liquid oozed down Greta's cheek and neck, and the toxic smell of peanut butter filled her nostrils. On her plate landed what could have been a moldy hamburger patty or what could also have been a rotten fish. Or just a mutated ball of peanut butter. There was no way for Greta to be certain.

Greta recuperated from the surprise attack quickly, wiping the goop off her face with the collar of her midnight-blue shirt. Unfortunately, this was not the first time a classmate had thrown an unidentified, rotting piece of food at her head. And sadly, Greta knew it probably wouldn't be the last.

She scanned the mess hall, looking for the aggressor.

She didn't have to look long.

"That's what you get for staring," Lola cackled. She turned back to her table and said, "She's just such an easy target."

"The easiest," Rox echoed with an exaggerated laugh.

Chopper gave Greta a smile that reminded her of a knife. "Bull's-eye."

Tashi rolled her eyes.

Sierra just petted her snake and kept quiet.

Greta knew better than to feed Lola's fire, but this time she couldn't help it. First the rotten BLASTketball practice and now the actual rotten food stuck to her face. It was just too much.

Lola's pitch was enough to start a full-blown food fight. It didn't take much. Moon Twins were always one cup of spilled soda away from a food war.

A handful of macaroni whizzed by Greta on the right. She ducked just in time to avoid an egg that someone must have stashed away.

Enough was enough.

Greta grabbed her leftover macaroni, squared her hips toward Lola (who was picking on another victim now), and wound up to throw.

"Lola, you're a psycho!" Greta screamed into the roar of the fight. Lola didn't seem to hear her.

Before the macaroni could leave her hand, something cold and wet hit the back of her head. As she turned in the direction of the attack, she slipped on a puddle of . . . something. Spilled juice? Barbecue sauce? Gravy?

It didn't matter. Greta went down hard, the handful of macaroni that was intended for Lola landing right on Greta's forehead. Grease and bright-orange cheese trickled into her eyes.

This was officially the worst day ever.

CHAPTER THREE

GLORIA

Gloria lay on her bed, staring up at the ceiling. A bad dream had woken her up soon after she'd fallen asleep. Though she couldn't remember the specifics, it left her with a gnawing, panicky feeling. She hadn't been able to fall back asleep since. Her mind lingered over the speech incident earlier that evening at the pep rally. How could she have been so foolish? Just suggesting that Sun School was in any way imperfect was practically treasonous, let alone trying to change it. Gloria was certain that if it hadn't been for her stellar academic record and dedication to the school as Sun Class President, she would have been expelled from Gemini Academy already.

But that didn't matter as much now, because her favorite time of week had come at last: Fraturday, when she would meet her Moon Twin sister, Greta, at Lake Vetiti.

Gloria had never been caught sneaking out of the dormitory. Not once. She liked to think it was because she was an above-average sneaker, a skill she'd started to take a tremendous amount of pride in. Though she couldn't do so publicly; it wasn't very Sun Twin, after all.

So, she was shocked when she heard an ever-so-quiet *psssst* as she tiptoed out of her room on the way to meet Greta that morning. She wore Gemini Academy–issued pajamas (golden yellow for Sun Twins, duh), and held her sneakers in one hand and a towel in the other. A baggie of organic carrot sticks bulged under her top.

"Where are you going?" Lana whispered from the next bed over. All seventh-grade Sun Twins slept in one long room, beds aligned opposite one another in two rows. Every bed came with one crisp white pillow, one soft yellow comforter, and, at nighttime, one peacefully sleeping Sun Twin.

Gloria stopped in her tracks and tried to act casual. "The . . . bathroom? I forgot to brush my teeth."

Would she fall for it?

Lana's big brown eyes blinked back at Gloria, her long, black hair waterfalling over her pillow. For a second, Gloria felt guilty for lying. Or trying to lie. She could always stop by the bathroom on the way out. Would that make it less of a lie? Or a white lie—was that right? They'd just learned the differ-ence between different types of lies in ethics class. Gloria didn't totally understand how there could be different levels of lying, but also, she hadn't been listening. Ethics class was an official snooze, as far as Gloria was concerned.

"Sneakers and a towel to brush your teeth?" Lana pulled her fluffy blanket up to her chin and yawned. "Also, it's five in the morning. You're just now remembering about your teeth?"

Shoot. Gloria shifted to make sure her towel concealed the carrots. For some reason Gloria simply could not understand, her twin sister just loved carrots. Greta often complained that the Moon School dining hall never served anything with nutritional value. Gloria was happy to bring her sister all the produce she could get her hands on. These days, carrots, and most other vegetables, tasted to Gloria like a combination of bark and dust.

Talk about no good deed going unpunished.

"Don't worry about it," Gloria whispered, eager to get moving. She didn't want to be too late. They only had one precious hour at Lake Vetiti. They had to make every second count. "Go back to sleep."

"Are you breaking the rules?" Lana asked, a little louder, eyes a little wider.

"Shhh!" Gloria hissed.

"*Are* you?"

"No! Of course not! No way! Rules are not meant to be broken!"

Gloria wasn't telling the truth, but she wasn't officially lying yet, either. Oh, well. All she knew was that rules were *fun* to break from time to time. Gloria didn't think that was something Lana would understand, though.

"Okeydokey. I didn't think so." Lana yawned again.

Gloria turned to go, but right before she did, Lana spoke once more. "But if you were, I wouldn't tell." Lana smiled, seemingly satisfied, and rolled over and went back to sleep.

Huh. That was weird, Gloria thought. She could have sworn she saw Lana give her a wink, too.

But she didn't have time to think about that now. Gloria silently crept out of the room, and glided down the peaceful hallway and out a tiny side door of Sun Dorm. Once outside, she galloped to the edge of the Great Lawn, entering the woods where a rock shaped like a top hat marked a concealed pathway. Finally free, she sprinted the entire way to Lake Vetiti. Her lungs burned, but she didn't slow down once.

CHAPTER FOUR

GRETA

Greta sat on a log at the edge of Lake Vetiti. The sky above was a vibrant mix of midnight blues, purples, and pinks—not quite night, but not quite sunrise, either. In the distance, Greta could see the tallest turrets of Gemini Academy poking above the trees. The main castle's stone exterior appeared gray in the still twilight.

For now.

Greta pushed her dark-blue pajama bottoms up to her knees and dangled her feet in the cool water. She was still sweating from her journey to the lake. It wasn't terribly far—just a dash across the Great Lawn, a sharp right into the woods at the top hat-shaped rock, then another few treacherous minutes dodging overgrown branches, fallen logs, and the occasional rodent—but Greta never dawdled. A slight tickle of fear encouraged her to sprint the entire way, so Greta always arrived at the lake winded and sweaty. Greta was tempted to jump into the water simply to cool off a bit, but she dutifully waited for her sister. She picked up one of the pearly rocks that lined the lake's shore, feeling its smooth, chilled surface in the palm of her hand. Instead of sand or mud, these peculiar rocks lined the shore and the bottom of Lake Vetiti. Greta threw the stone into the water. It skipped one . . . two . . . three . . . four times before sinking into the lake.

Lake Vetiti was Greta's favorite place in the world. The water was always the perfect temperature (refreshing, but not chilly), the air always smelled the way that air should smell (pine trees and honeysuckle), but most of all, it felt private. And special. And it made Greta feel adventurous. Daring. Like a bona fide Moon Twin.

"If only Lola could see me now," Greta said to herself triumphantly, checking her watch.

Gloria was late. Again. She always insisted on arriving anywhere from five to eight minutes late (not very Sun Twin–like), so Greta was used to having a few minutes to herself at the lake before her sister arrived.

Lake Vetiti was the one place Sun Twins and Moon Twins alike were forbidden from going, and it was the only rule that even all Moon Twins obeyed—including Lola. Greta and Gloria had discovered it several years ago and purely by accident. Fraturday meetings used to convene at the abandoned toolshed in the woods that stood between Gemini Academy and the lake. This was back during Gloria's "Let's pretend the ground is lava" phase. After nearly forty-five minutes of darting around the woods, swinging from low-hanging branches, and jumping from fallen log to tree stump, the sisters found themselves standing on the shore of Lake Vetiti.

It had been their Fraturday meeting spot ever since.

Greta heard some rustling in the shrubs behind her. Then some crashing. And then silence.

Gloria.

Greta counted to five. She kept her eyes out on the lake and grinned. She knew what was coming.

"Boo!" Gloria exclaimed, crashing through the bushes and grabbing Greta's shoulders.

Greta didn't flinch. What Gloria overlooked when trying to surprise her Moon Twin sister was that Greta was accustomed to sudden sneak attacks. Moon Twins loved to sneak up on you for no reason when you least expected it.

Instead, she smiled and turned around to hug her Sun Twin. "Hey, sis."

"Scare ya?" Gloria asked as they embraced.

"Not a chance," Greta answered.

"Ooh, one of these days . . ."

"If you're lucky," Greta said with a wink.

Suddenly, Gloria pulled out of the hug. "Are you wearing perfume?" she asked quizzically. Before Greta could speak, Gloria answered her own question. "Another BLASTketball went off, I assume?"

Greta sighed. She thought she'd managed to get the stink off her in the shower.

"Okay, tell me all about it," Gloria said. "But not here. In the water!"

And with that, Gloria kicked off her shoes and stripped down to her bathing suit. Greta did the same. She dove into the water right behind her Sun Twin.

After a few minutes, Gloria told Greta about her speech and the catastrophic aftermath.

"It was like I had suggested we stop saying *please* and *thank you* or something," Gloria complained. "They were all so offended, especially Headmistress Solis."

"Hmm," Greta said, considering the possibility.

Greta floated on her back while Gloria stood in the chest-deep water. Gloria wasn't a floater. Greta suspected her sister would be pacing if water allowed for such brisk movement.

"And you know the worst part?" Gloria asked, annoyed.

"What?"

Gloria whispered now. "I *still* think I'm right. It'd be so worth it. Adding one extra on-theme art project hardly counts as a major change to the fair. This would *never* have happened at Moon School!"

"Definitely," Greta agreed. Except for the BLASTketball game, Moon Twin activities were different every year. She'd always wondered why Sun School insisted upon the same Sun activities for the fair every year. What a snooze.

"Ugh," Gloria yelled. "It was so embarrassing, Greta!"

"I promise you, it couldn't have been worse than my BLASTketball practice today."

"The more I think about it," Gloria began, "the less I under-stand why that crazy coach of yours has you all bullying each other all the time."

"Because how *else* are you supposed to score?" Greta made her best impression of Coach Sliver.

"What about passing?" Gloria asked.

"The point is to win, Glo, not to—" Greta was getting nowhere. "Never mind."

"No, tell me. What is it?"

"I . . . I just don't know what to do anymore," Greta said, slamming her fist into the water, the splash emphasizing her point.

The two sisters were silent for a moment, Greta floating on her back, Gloria treading water by her side. They gazed up at the sky. Even in the dark, Greta could tell there were storm clouds building overhead.

"If it stinks so much, why don't you just quit?" Gloria sug-gested, finally.

Greta shook her head. "No matter how hard I try, I just can't seem to fit in at Moon School."

Gloria started as if she were about to speak, but stopped before any words formed. Instead, she took her sister's hand in hers. The girls floated on their backs, side by side, and for the first time since last Fraturday, Greta wanted to stay exactly where she was.

"Tell me about that Medieval Torture class again," Gloria said finally.

"You are *such* a bad Sun Twin!" Greta teased. Gloria had become increasingly curious about her Moon Twin's curriculum recently.

"Yeah, yeah. I can only handle so much kittens and embroidery."

"I'd take sweet baby animals over vipers and scorpions any day." Greta shivered. She hated reptiles almost more than she hated Lola.

Almost.

"Don't change the subject!" Gloria chanted.

"Okay, fine, you weirdo. This week, Mrs. Hastam went on and on about the Chair of Torture. Apparently, it was very innovative because it had spikes on the armrests, footrests, *and* seat."

"Whoa. Brutal," Gloria said.

"Mrs. Hastam doesn't like me, though. She gave me a D on my midterm."

"Yikes. It's so weird that you guys get grades. If you did your work, why are you being punished?" Gloria asked.

"Because I answered all the questions wrong." *Duh*, Greta thought.

"What's worse: getting the wrong answers or smelling like an exploded BLASTketball all day long?" Gloria teased.

"Well, both are very bad," Greta said, splashing Gloria with lake water.

"Hey!" Gloria cried, splashing back. In no time, Gloria and Greta were in the middle of a full-on splash fight. But it didn't last for long. Pretty soon they dissolved into uncontrollable giggles.

Greta didn't mind when Gloria teased her. Gloria's laughter felt completely different from when Lola and the other Moon Twins made fun of her. Their snickers felt like kicks in the stomach, but Gloria's giggles always reminded Greta of hugs, somehow.

After their swim, the girls sat on the shore, gazing at the lake. Soft flecks of sunlight dotted the surface of the water. It was almost dawn. Almost time to go.

Greta wrapped herself in Gloria's towel and munched noisily on a carrot. Gloria preferred to air dry.

"Moon School is officially worse than ever this year," Greta complained.

Greta reached for a carrot. She liked the way the vegetable crunched between her teeth. She could practically feel the vitamins seeping into her.

"Don't worry about Mrs. Hastam. She sounds mean."

"It's not just her. The only class I'm not totally failing is Breaking and Entering, which is, like, the most pointless class ever if you don't have plans to become a criminal, which I obviously don't. I'm hopeless at BLASTketball, I officially don't have any friends, and Lola . . ." Greta paused and shuddered. "She's just the *worst*. She called me a Sun Twin today. In front of *everyone*."

"That's rough," said Gloria. "Sun School is no walk in the park, either. Everything bores me out of my mind. Every day it's the same thing, over and over again."

"Well, except for last night."

"Ugh, don't remind me," Gloria said. "I can't believe I embarrassed myself in front of the entire Sun School student body. I don't know if I'll ever live it down, to be honest."

"Well, what can we do?" Greta asked, taking a bite out of a carrot stick.

"I dunno," Gloria said softly. "I think you gotta stand up for yourself, Greta."

"And I think you need to follow your instincts, Glo. Make a change for yourself."

The sisters sighed together. They were both right.

Then they said, "I wish you could just do it for me."

CHAPTER FIVE

GLORIA

Gloria looked at her sister in disbelief.

"That's it!" Gloria exclaimed, jumping to her feet. Her heartbeat increased, and her armpits tingled the way they always did when something exciting was about to happen.

"What is?" Greta asked, confused.

"Why *don't* you just do it for me? Why don't we just do it for *one another*?"

"Huh?"

"Why don't *I* go to Moon School for you, and you go to Sun School for me?"

Greta looked at Gloria skeptically.

"Think about it!" Gloria was onto something, and she knew it. "You need help standing up for yourself, and I'd rather do anything than face all the Sun Twins and plan a fair after that brutal pep rally."

By the time Gloria finished her thought, Greta was on her feet, too, gripping Gloria's hands in hers. Their eyes met, and suddenly they were both very, very quiet.

"We're twins, after all! Who would even notice? I really think—" Gloria whispered, unable to finish her sentence.

"Maybe." Greta sounded as serious as Gloria had ever heard her. "We would have to be—"

"Careful, I know—"

"It's never been—"

"We would be—"

"How could we—"

Just then, a ray of sun shot over the lake and illuminated Greta's Moon Charm. For a moment, the crescent glimmered like a diamond. Gloria brought her hand to her neck and clutched her own Sun Charm.

"Our charms!" The girls exclaimed at the same time.

Suddenly, they both knew what they had to do.

CHAPTER SIX

GRETA

Greta fastened the clasp on Gloria's necklace. Gloria turned around, and the twins faced each other. Greta now wore yellow pajamas and a Sun Charm; Gloria was in midnight-blue pajamas and had a Moon Charm around her neck.

Greta held the Sun Charm in her fist. It was different from what she was used to. Still unusually cool and incredibly smooth, but also bigger. Rounder.

"Just for a week," Gloria said. "When you return to Moon School, you'll no longer be the laughingstock. You'll see." Gloria sounded confident, but Greta still looked at her sister skeptically. "Trust me."

"Okay." If Greta trusted anyone, it was her twin sister. "And I'll take care of fair planning for you."

"And?"

"And get everybody to see that change is not a bad thing." Gloria looked at her with raised eyebrows. "I will, Glo. I really will."

"That's what I like to hear," Gloria said with a grin. Then, in a whisper, "I really think it will work. We'll switch back next Fraturday. Easy as that!"

"What if I need to talk to you before then? Like if something goes wrong?"

Greta waited for Gloria to respond, to come up with the solution.

"Notes! We can leave each other notes! Right under that big top hat–shaped rock that marks the path into the woods."

"Okay. But you have to remember to check."

"I will," Gloria said.

Greta believed her.

"You don't think we'll get caught, do you?" Greta asked. Now that the idea was becoming real, she was starting to get nervous. This was a very big risk. If they got caught, who knew what might happen to them?

"How would we get caught?" Gloria asked. "Really, think about it. We're identical twins."

They turned to look at their reflections in the lake. Same kind-of-curly, kind-of-straight, shoulder-length cinnamon hair; same solitary freckle on their right cheek; same bottom tooth that stood slightly taller than the rest. Gloria was right; they *were* the same, at least on the outside. Now that they'd switched charms, there was no way to know that Greta was Gloria, and Gloria was Greta. Except . . .

"But what if—"

"Don't worry. It'll be easy for you. Just fake it till you make it," Gloria interrupted, reading her mind.

Just then, another sharp ray of light shot across the lake. "We have to go," said Gloria.

Gloria took off through the woods, and Greta sprinted behind her. Her mind whirled. They were really doing it! They'd really switched places.

They stopped next to the top-hat rock at the edge of the woods.

"Good luck," Gloria said breathlessly. "Don't be scared."

Did Greta look scared? Sometimes Greta didn't need to explain anything; her sister just understood. "Just follow Lana, Aisha, and Daisy. Lana is, like, the sweetest Sun Twin ever."

"Who are they?"

"My friends, dummy."

Friends. Greta suddenly had friends. Immediately, she stood a little taller.

The sisters hugged.

"Love you, Sun Twin," Greta whispered.

"Love you back, Moon Twin."

There they parted ways—Gloria to bed with the other Moon Twins, and Greta to breakfast with the other Sun Twins.

As twilight faded into sunrise, a beam of sunlight shone upon the gray stone walls of Gemini Academy. In an instant, the light washed away the last remnants of Moon School, peeling back the gray stone and stubborn vines to reveal polished marble that gleamed for all to see. From the nearby forest, birds, butterflies, and other small woodland animals ventured from their nests and burrows, replacing the bats and rabid raccoons that had prowled the campus the night before. From puddles and mud sprouted soft green grass and plucky tulips. The storm that had seemed so menacing just a few hours ago subsided and made way for a radiant blue sky.

And the enormous crest that sat above Gemini Academy's spectacular entryway, with its sparkling crescent moon insignia—the symbol of Moon School—melted away to welcome the Sun School crest: a bright sun that shimmered in the morning light.

Indeed, a new day had begun.

CHAPTER SEVEN

GLORIA

Gloria wiggled into the covers, kicking the top sheet to a clump at the bottom of the bed. So far, Moon Dorm seemed exactly the same as Sun Dorm. Well, minus the fact that she was in a basement with only tiny slits at the top of the walls for windows. And the fact that every Moon Twin down there was snoring.

There was one thing Gloria hadn't admitted to her sister back at the lake. Her idea to switch had sparked a curiosity that felt simultaneously important and frightening. If Gloria had felt less like herself for the past two months, two weeks, and almost three days in Sun School, then might she feel better—or more like herself—at Moon School? That was a lot to think about. Too much for right now, for Gloria was sleepy.

Ah, sleep. This switch was already working in her favor. First period at Sun School would begin any minute, but Gloria had an extra stretch of slumber ahead of her. And the Moon Dorms really were the perfect place for it: dark, cool, and subterranean.

As she climbed into Greta's bed, Gloria stretched into a giant X and drifted into a deep, dreamless sleep.

CHAPTER EIGHT

GRETA

Once Greta's eyes adjusted to the dark, Gloria's bed wasn't hard to find. Messy, messy, messy. Again, very un–Sun Twin of Gloria. What looked like several Sun School uniforms peeked out from under the bed. Gloria's standard-issue Gemini Academy trunk stood open at the foot of her bed. More dirty clothes spilled over the sides.

How does she live like this? Greta wondered.

That would be her first order of business—to tidy things up. How was she expected to get Gloria's life together while living in a pigsty? But she needed rest. Until now, Greta had neglected to consider that the switch would lose her a night of sleep.

Greta tucked herself under the covers and pulled them up to her chin. Whoa. Was it just her, or was Sun School bedding fluffier, softer, and altogether more pleasant? This was definitely not the hard mattress she had gotten used to for the past seven years. No wonder Gloria had baby-soft skin.

As she cozied under the blanket, Greta's breath steadied. They'd done it. They'd really done it. For the first time in a long, long time, Greta felt relaxed. She wrapped her hand around her new Sun Charm and closed her eyes. The peaceful breaths of the seventh-grade Sun Twins around her soothed her to sleep.

But Greta awoke only a few minutes later to the sound of music. It was soft and light and reminded her of beauty.

"Rise and shine, sleepyhead," someone said in the next bed over. Natural light spilled in from the tall windows, splashing tall rectangles of sunshine over the sleeping hall.

Greta turned toward the voice and gasped. There lay Lola, smiling sweetly. But no, it wasn't Lola. Something was different. The yellow sheets, the high ceilings, the fluffy mattress . . . this wasn't Lola—it must have been her twin.

The girl was sitting up now, combing her long, black hair out with her fingers. Sunshine made the flecks of gold in her eyes dance. Whoa. This was going to take some getting used to. The girl seemed so . . . sweet. And not the kind of sweet that would suddenly turn rotten and stab you in the back. *Nice* sweet. But what was this girl's name? Greta couldn't just ask Lola's Sun Twin what her name was—that would be super suspicious. Lola's twin and Gloria were friends. If only she could remember Gloria's friends' names! Greta had to think quickly. She looked all around her. Maybe there was something with the girl's name on it, a hairbrush or a notebook or . . . a trunk!

"Rise and shine," Greta said, repeating the phrase she'd never before heard but assumed had something to do with waking up. She stood up and walked over to the foot of their beds, where she could see a golden nameplate on the girl's Sun School trunk. It read LANA LEWIS. Yup, definitely Lola's twin.

Greta sighed with relief, but her head still felt foggy. Was it all the sunshine? She blinked. It was calm here. After the alarm sounded at Moon School, the dorm was always filled with grumbling, moaning, and pleas to go back to sleep. And it was never this quiet and bright outside when Moon Twins woke up. It was nighttime, and there was always a thunderstorm raging over the academy grounds.

"I don't know how my hair gets so knotty overnight! I'm just sleeping," Lana said. "How'd you sleep, Glo?" Her smile was kind and inviting. "You were so quiet last night."

Greta's stomach flipped. Quiet? Lana was supposed to be sleeping; how would she know if Greta was quiet? Did Lana notice Greta quietly sneak back in? Greta scrambled to come up with an excuse as to why she'd been awake in the wee hours of the morning. *I just got up to use the bathroom.* Would that work? It would have to, right? Anyone might have to use the bathroom in the middle of the night, right? Or was that only a Moon Twin thing?

Greta felt herself starting to panic. She grasped her Sun Charm around her neck. *Relax,* she thought. *She can't know.* What would Gloria say?

"I was, um . . ." Greta finally squeaked.

"You didn't wake me up more than once. Maybe you finally got all that snoring out of your system," Lana joked.

Greta let out the longest, sweetest exhale.

She was safe. Snoring. That's right, her sister snored.

"Don't forget your toothbrush," Lana said again, cheerfully, with a wink.

Wow. Gloria wasn't kidding. Sun Twins really *were* just altogether nice and helpful. Reminding her to bring her toothbrush to the bathroom! Now *that* was just downright considerate.

Greta took a long, deep inhale. This was going to be a good day. Great, even.

With a smile on her face, Greta skipped toward the bathroom, ready to embrace her inner Sun Twin.

The short walk from Sun Dorm to the dining hall had been fascinating. Greta knew the way, of course. The buildings were all in the same place, though Sun Dorm was on the opposite side of the castle. As far as Greta could tell, the structure and layout of the school was familiar, but otherwise everything looked . . . different. It was like seeing an old friend in a brand-new costume.

The air outside smelled fresh and clean. At first, the relentless sunshine hurt Greta's eyes, but after a few minutes she got used to it. Sunshine was simply the best thing ever! How had she gone so long in Moon School without it? Despite such little sleep, Greta felt more and more energized with each breath she took. Perfectly manicured grass lined the pathway from the dorms to the dining hall. Butterflies floated through the air and birds chirped all around. Unlike at Moon School, none of the stones that marked the path to the dining hall were missing or wobbly, and the ground was covered in a lush layer of grass instead of dead weeds and mud.

Greta let out a sigh of relief that turned into a light laugh. Gloria was right: She *was* going to be fine.

"What's so funny?" Lana asked when she noticed Greta's— or, well, *Gloria*'s—smile.

Greta told her the truth: "What a beautiful, marvelous day!"

Lana smiled and linked her arm through Greta's. "I'm so glad to hear it! Especially after what happened at the pep rally."

Together, they skipped toward breakfast. Greta giggled with utter delight. She couldn't help it. Sun School simply inspired joy, happiness, and whatever word meant the opposite of lonely.

The dining hall smelled like freshly baked bread. Greta took a deep breath and took in her surroundings. More sunshine poured in through the tall windows. When she looked up, the bats that she had become accustomed to in Moon

73

School were missing. The ceiling was painted a light blue that looked like the sky, and a soft rainbow cascaded across from one corner to the other. Rows of long, light wood tables stood throughout the room in perfect order. In chairs with plump white cushions sat perfectly pleasant Sun Twins.

Following Lana to a table, Greta carried a yellow tray with two sunny-side up eggs, a piping hot roll, a slice of cantaloupe in the shape of a smile, and a tall glass of orange juice.

This is heaven, Greta thought. *Dining hall heaven.*

Greta followed Lana to the table where Daisy and Aisha were waiting.

Whenever Gloria had talked about her friends, Greta had had a hard time paying attention. Especially as of late, Gloria had made them all sound exactly the same: cheerful, sweet, and boring.

But Gloria couldn't have been more wrong. Well, about the boring part, that is. Yup, Aisha, Daisy, and Lana were anything but boring—they were too nice to be boring! After Lana generously reminded her to brush her teeth, Aisha had given Greta a big hug when she first saw her in the morning. Daisy had already complimented Greta on her hair (it was just in a ponytail) and how rested she looked (which seemed impossible, but Greta wasn't going to question her).

"So," Lana said, sliding into the seat next to her. "Let's get down to some Gemini Academy Fair business. Divide and conquer!"

It dawned on Greta that when it was Moon School's turn, she still had no idea who was responsible for setting up the fair. There wasn't a Moon School Class President; that would require a Moon Twin to be, well, responsible. Being involved with this whole planning thing was nice. Greta suddenly understood why predictability was so valued over here in Sun School.

Lana pulled out four pieces of pale yellow paper and four perfectly sharpened No. 2 pencils and passed them around. The top of the page read *Gemini Academy Fair: Sun Twin Checklist!* in perfect green lettering.

"Cool font." Greta said. She'd never seen this one before. The letters were all so . . . precise.

Lana giggled. "My handwriting, silly. I'm still trying to perfect my *s*. I can't seem to get the curves equally curvy every time, if you know what I mean."

But Greta didn't know what she meant. The *s* looked like an *s* to her. She didn't see the problem.

"The *s* is great. Perfect."

Lana waved off the tribute, though Greta could see her rosy cheeks flush to a slightly richer shade of dark pink. "You're sweet."

Sweet. Greta was sweet. And Lana meant it as a compliment, not an insult.

Greta sat up a little bit straighter. She was ready to take the lead.

"So. The checklist!" Greta looked down at the paper and read the first item. *"Number one: Pick a theme."*

"Check!" Aisha said, writing a check mark in the little box next to the item. Greta did the same. She felt accomplished already. *"Sharing Is Caring* has such a nice ring to it."

"A beautiful ring," Daisy chimed in.

"Item number two: Decorations!" Greta read aloud. She noticed that the checklist only had four items: theme, decorations, setup, and concessions. Surely one could keep track of those four things without a checklist, but in that moment, it dawned on Greta how happy she was to have everything spelled out in list form.

"My favorite part!" Daisy said, clapping her hands together.

"So, we'll need flowers everywhere—not just in the flower-arranging stations, but in vases to use as accents in other booths." Aisha said excitedly. "The accent vases looked so great two years ago."

"Yeah, I loved that part, too," Daisy said, before using her fork and knife to cut off a slice of egg white. Greta, suddenly self-conscious, looked down at the melon in her hands. She quickly returned it to the plate and picked up her fork and knife. She hadn't used eating utensils in *years*. They felt both clumsy and comfortable in her hands. She did her best to look natural while cutting pieces of melon.

"Ugh, I just love flowers so much, I really do," Lana said,

wiping a small smear of jelly from her lip with a crisp white napkin. "How about if you and I do the trimming, and Aisha and Daisy, you can put them in their vases? Does that sound good, Glo?"

Greta took a bite of melon. It was delicious. She washed it down with a gulp of orange juice.

"Sure." Greta really did think flowers were great. But how else could they maximize their aesthetic contribution? "Gemini Academy Fair is about 'bonding and reminding the Sun Twin community of the value of working together and friendship,'" Greta said, carefully quoting the poster on the wall next to their table.

"Oh, it just hit me!" Daisy said, raising her hand in the air as if she were in class. "You know how we always have yellow streamers, and we braid those streamers? That braid totally fits with the theme. Like, braids totally symbolize togetherness, don't you think?"

"Without a doubt," Aisha said. "Good one, Daisy, you really—"

"Who wants to do all the braiding?" Greta asked. She was getting the hang of things already. Divide and conquer. Such an effective strategy!

Nobody answered right away.

After a moment, Lana spoke. "Glo, you should apologize to Aisha for interrupting her."

Greta was puzzled. She didn't know that interrupting was something you had to apologize for. Wasn't that just the way people talked?

"My bad. Sorry, Aisha."

"It's okay. Thank you for your apology," Aisha said with a smile.

And just like that, they picked up where they left off.

"Daisy, you want to ask Ms. Joy to donate participation stickers? She always gives out the best participation stickers," Lana said.

"You bet!" Daisy was so excited, she was bouncing up and down in her seat. "Everybody loved those two years ago!"

"Aisha, do you mind making the flower crowns again?" asked Lana.

"Of course! You know how much I love a flower crown!"

Greta didn't think it was worth pointing out that the theme was about sharing and caring, and not necessarily flowers. Daisy, Aisha, and Lana continued to divvy up tasks. Greta noticed that each suggestion included the phrases *like two years ago* or *in the past*.

Things were going well. Greta remembered Gloria's idea about the community painting, and thought now might be a safe time to bring it back up. Greta was about to when she felt a gentle tap on her shoulder. She turned around to find a small girl staring up at her. The small girl must have been

Sierra's Sun Twin. Greta hoped she didn't also have a pet reptile.

"Hello. You guys are planning for the fair, right?"

"Yes," said Greta.

"May I help?"

Greta looked back at her friends. She imagined Lola and her gang. Once, way back in second grade, Greta had asked if she could help them play blocks. They were building super-high towers, and then they took turns knocking them down, all the blocks scattering to the ground in a heap. Greta had just wanted to help them reorganize the blocks before the next build. The disorganization of the pile on the floor made her breath quicken to an uncomfortable pace when she looked at it for too long. When Greta had asked, Lola had thrown a block at her and told her to go away.

Greta hadn't thought about that in a long time.

Aisha, Daisy, and Lana met Greta's gaze. Greta didn't know what the clique rules were like in Sun School. Would her friends have a problem if this other girl joined them? Was that something Gloria would allow? Greta turned back to the newcomer. Before she could speak, Lana beat her to it.

"Okeydokey, of course, Mitten. Please, sit down!"

Mitten. What an odd yet perfectly suited name. Greta now noticed that Mitten had pulled an extra chair over with her. Lana scooted over and Mitten pushed her seat in between them.

"Where were we?" Aisha asked.

"Well, I guess we were still technically on item number two. I don't know if this falls into the decorations category or the concessions category," Lana said. She furrowed her brow as she looked at her checklist. Decorations was number two; concessions was number four. "I think if we just get to the concessions booth a little early, we'll have plenty of time to organize the snack presentation by food group, right?"

"Totally," Greta confirmed. "So, I know it didn't go over so well yesterday, but I was thinking about the theme and the group mural painting idea again—"

The girls all gasped. Daisy covered her mouth with her hand. Aisha almost dropped her juice cup. Mitten nibbled on her thumbnail and didn't blink. Then, Lana cleared her throat.

"Gloria," Lana whispered. "You really have to drop that."

"I say this with utmost respect and compassion, but this really is *not* a good idea," Aisha said seriously.

"Not good." Daisy was nearly hyperventilating at this point. "Risky, I'd say."

"Yeah, with the Moon Twins there, they'd surely sabotage the project in some way I don't even want to think about," Aisha added.

Greta took a bite of eggs. The two bright-yellow yolks started back at her, unbroken, like lanterns. Or eyeballs. This was going to be harder than she thought.

She had to give them more time.

"You all, I was just kidding." Her friends shifted in their seats. Mitten continued to stare at her plate. "Keeping you on your toes!"

They all nodded and suddenly became very interested in their food.

"Another time. A group drawing or art piece would be fun. Another time," Mitten said suddenly.

"How do you even do a drawing as a group? All share a crayon or something?" Aisha asked, giggling. Then Daisy giggled with her. Greta didn't know what was so funny.

"No, you don't share the paintbrush or marker or whatever, just the canvas. It's kind of like art and improvisation at the same time," Mitten said. The more Greta looked at Mitten, the more the peculiar name felt fitting.

"Improvisation sounds very Moon Twin," Daisy warned.

"And, like . . . what kind of stuff are you supposed to draw?" Aisha asked.

"It could be anything," Mitten said. "Anything you want."

"Interesting," Aisha said.

Really interesting, Greta thought to herself. She didn't express herself out loud. It was only her first few hours in Sun School. Best not raise any suspicion by showing curiosity about an idea that seemed so out of the ordinary.

"I don't get it," Daisy said flatly.

"Hmm," Lana began, "it sounds like—"

But she was interrupted by the most beautiful music. It

reminded Greta of twinkling lights or a delicate waterfall. Everyone around her started to get up and clear their places. *That must be the bell*, Greta thought. It was so different from Moon School's bloodcurdling scream that sounded between classes. It almost always caught Greta by surprise and sent a chill down her spine.

Greta went to pick up her tray when she noticed that somehow one of her yolks had broken. A thick, warm yellow oozed over the plate. It didn't look right. Greta tossed her napkin over her tray and stood up to clear her place.

Aside from the group painting fiasco, day one as a Sun Twin continued to be great.

Sun Teachers and Sun Twins alike were all about positive reinforcement. At first, Greta had been skeptical. When called on in geometry class (turned out the angles in a triangle *always* added up to 180 degrees—how great!) she knew that she'd answered a few questions incorrectly. In Intro to Botany, she'd forgotten to read the instructions and made a mess of her experiment. Still, everyone just kept focusing on the positive, saying things like, *Good try, Glo, you were only a few degrees off in the triangle measurement!* and *No biggie, the beaker just overflowed onto the table, not onto the floor! I'll help you clean it up.* After a few periods, Greta was starting to feel right at home.

And it just kept getting better.

During gym, they played a rousing game of basketball. Ordinary basketball—lots of teamwork and no detonators. And Greta thrived. Sun Twins did this thing called "passing"— a smart, kind, and incredibly effective tactic. Even though her first pass was intercepted, Coach Valentine had shouted, "Great idea, Gloria!" After a few more minutes of carefully observing the action, she learned she was a master passer. *Why punch when you can pass?* she realized. She couldn't wait to try this new tactic out when she got back to Moon School. For a second she missed shooting, and it definitely felt counterintuitive not to keep score, but passing and getting the ball farther up the court so efficiently was just so satisfying, she forgot her qualms quickly. After the scrimmage, the two sides lined up at half-court and went down the line, giving each other high fives and saying things like, *Awesome job!*, *Great teamwork!*, and, Greta's favorite, *Good game!*

By the last class of the day, some complicated sort of poetry course, Greta had noticed a trend. The scoreless basketball game had tipped her off. No wonder Gloria never complained about her grades or flubbing a big test. There weren't any grades in Sun School! She got back a math quiz that Gloria had taken before the switch, and instead of an A or a B (or C or D), there was just a bright-yellow sun sticker on the upper right corner. Greta snuck a peek at the girl sitting next to her; she had the same thing. That's when Greta noticed that everyone had one.

After dinner (another delightful, well-rounded meal), Greta hung back, making the excuse that she wanted to compliment the cook. Once the coast was clear, Greta darted out of the dining hall, across the field, and to the edge of the woods. She sat on top-hat rock and prepared to write a note to her sister.

There were so many things Greta wanted to tell Gloria right away. Like how nice it was to walk down the halls between classes without getting jostled or tripped. How it made her blush (but in a good way) every time she was complimented or encouraged (which was often). How much less lonely she was after just one day of having friends to chat with during mealtimes. But Greta didn't want to rub it in. Gloria would soon wake up to her first day at Moon School. Greta trusted that her sister could take care of herself, but still. Moon School was no plush walk in the park.

Greta quickly jotted a note to her sister on the back of the checklist, which, regrettably, was all she had in her pocket.

Glo—

Things are going great! Sun School is so fun. Why would you ever want to leave? Also, look at this checklist Lana made—we'll have Gemini Academy Fair planned in no time! Good luck in Moon School!

Love, G

Greta folded the paper into even quarters (as she had watched Lana do at the end of breakfast) and slipped it under the rock. As Greta trotted back across the field to Sun Dorm, nearly lightheaded from an unfamiliar sense of self-confidence, she remembered what she was there to do. She hadn't really made all that much progress as far as the mural project went. But she was allowed one day of fun, right? She'd start in on her plan tomorrow. Which reminded her: She needed a plan. Greta was just going to have to get creative. Show them that a little competition could be fun. Luckily, she had spent nearly seven years in Moon School. She suspected she was up to the task.

Greta noticed the mud on her shoe as she stepped into Sun Dorm. Where had that come from? She looked behind her, and just outside the door was a slightly wet spot in the path. How did that get there? As far as she knew, it never rained at Sun School. *Oh, well*, she thought, taking off her shoes so as not to track dirt inside the spotless entryway. Coming from a world of gloom and rain, Greta was accustomed to a little mud.

CHAPTER NINE
GLORIA

Gloria shot upright in bed. Her covers were tangled around her feet. The back of her neck was damp with sweat, her hair matted and tangled. Something frightening—something truly terrifying—had woken her up. A nightmare? Someone, or something, had been howling . . .

Then she heard it again: a bloodcurdling scream. The scream of someone scared for their life.

Gloria yelped. She looked around frantically, willing her eyes to adjust quickly to the dark.

The Moon Twins around her started to groan and kick under their sheets.

"Ten more minutes," someone called.

"Why do we have to get up so early?" another moaned.

Then it clicked: The scream was the alarm. It was just after sundown. Time to start the Moon School day . . . or night, rather. Gloria flopped back on her bed and smiled. *Very clever,* she thought.

Gloria put her feet onto the floor and stretched her arms overhead. She looked up as the candles on the large iron candelabra overhead lit out of nowhere. The small flames bathed the room in low, flickering light. It would have looked cozy had it not been for the cold, gray stone walls surrounding them.

Despite the absolutely chilling wake-up call, Gloria had had one of the best sleeps of her life. Now, she was ready to get the day started. *Moon School, here I come.*

"I think I liked you better when you *didn't* snore." Gloria looked up, confused. A girl in the bed next to hers rubbed her eyes and yawned. "You sounded like a bulldozer or something last night."

Gosh, it sure is easy to get on someone's bad side over here, Gloria thought.

Suddenly, something icy cold grabbed Gloria's ankle. She screamed. She screamed very loudly.

"Gotcha!" A girl with a long braid and threatening bangs emerged from under Gloria's bed. Then, she scuttled off, presumably to hide under another bed to scare the daylights out of another Moon Twin. Gloria noticed a small green snake the length of her shoe slithering behind the ankle grabber.

"Sharkbite! Has anyone seen Sharkbite?!" someone called from across the room. Gloria looked around frantically. Was there a pool of water filled with sharks that she had somehow missed? Hard to tell; the beds were scattered around with no apparent logic or order.

"That's the dumbest name for a toothless snake ever!" someone else called.

Gloria looked to the floor; the snake was out of sight.

"Sharkbite! Come here, Sharkbite!"

"Be quiet, Sierra!"

"Who asked you?"

"Did someone steal my shoe?"

"SHARKBITE!"

"I found your shoe!"

"SHARKBITE! I'M WARNING YOU!"

"That's not my shoe!"

Gloria didn't know where to look. This was pandemonium. As the volume and mixture of voices increased, the girl in the bed next to her started to jump up and down on her springy mattress.

"Cannonball!" Gloria's bed neighbor screamed as she soared through the air, nearly colliding with Gloria. Gloria threw her hands in front of her, blocking her face in case of a collision. When she looked up, the girl was already gone, jumping on a different bed now.

So this is how things went down in Moon School. *Alright*, Gloria thought. *Let the games begin.*

There was nothing that Greta could have said or done to prepare Gloria for Moon School. It was simply beyond imagination.

First, teeth brushing appeared to be completely optional. Gloria found herself the only one in the bathroom doing so. She was all about living the Moon Twin life, but not brushing your teeth? Ew.

Uniforms: also apparently optional. Moon Twins got dressed in the midnight-blue shorts and matching shirt, but that's about where the uniformity ended. Gloria had forgotten that clothing could be so expressive. Back in Sun School they wore the same uniform but in yellow, and shirts were always tucked in, all fabric clean and wrinkle-free. As everyone got dressed, Gloria noticed that one girl had the sleeves ripped off her blue shirt. Another had sewn extra pockets all over the front and back of her shorts (Gloria could only imagine what was in those pockets). Another girl wore a belt made of barbed wire and frayed rope. And yet another's whole outfit was so dirty, so stained, that it hardly looked blue at all.

Gloria took the cue and untucked her shirt. It felt . . . weirdly nice. *Let's go with this*, she thought. The collar on the silly school–issued shirts had always annoyed her. It made things hot and seemed to serve no real purpose. Before she could second-guess herself, Gloria ripped the collar clean off her shirt. The tear sounded like freedom.

This was going to be fun.

When Gloria got to the mess hall for breakfast, she was sweaty, muddy, and hungry.

Getting from the Moon Dorm to the mess hall proved to be an exerting journey. Moon Twins liked to race, it seemed. Race to the dorm exit, race down the stone path that led to the main castle, race to jump in the nearest puddle, race down the halls funneling to the dining hall. When Gloria paused to take in the Moon School crest above the entrance to the main castle, she was nearly trampled. The fact that it was almost as dark inside as it was outside didn't help steady her footing, either. But Gloria had kept up. Nothing like a borderline obstacle course to start off the day. At least it was more eventful than what she was used to in the morning.

Gloria surveyed the mess hall after she'd picked up her tray of food. Unlike Sun School, where everyone got the same tray with the same meal, Moon School had choices. There was a hot food station serving pancakes and meat of unknown origin, and then a big table with boxes and boxes of chocolate and brightly colored, sugary cereals. Gloria grabbed a stack of pancakes and decided to go for it with the cereal; she put a little bit of each kind in a giant bowl and filled it with chocolate milk. *Go big or go home*, she thought.

The layout of the tables in the mess hall didn't follow any particular logic that Gloria could see. Gloria found an empty seat and sat down. She had to resist the instinct to sit with others. Greta did not have friends—at least that's what Greta always told her. Gloria had yet to discover Greta's enemies—the savage-sounding Lola girl and her crew hadn't revealed themselves yet—so she played it safe and enjoyed her breakfast on her own.

And enjoy she did. It didn't matter that there didn't seem to be a single spoon in the building; Gloria followed suit and shoveled slurpy scoops of cereal into her mouth with her hand. It didn't take her long to realize that the low but constant smacking sounds all around her were Moon Twins chewing their food with their mouths wide open. Gloria tried it. It was fun. A few bites of food fell out of her mouth and onto her shirt. Gloria paused and looked around. Nobody stopped her or looked twice. So she did it again. And again. And again.

She ate her entire breakfast that way.

The journey from the dining hall to the first class of the day was just as frantic as before; everyone was on a sugar high from breakfast. Gloria felt like she was in some sort of super-fast haunted house. She couldn't see more than a few feet ahead of her; the hallways were dimly lit with flickering bare light bulbs that hung loosely from the ceiling. On the way to first period, while she was trying to untangle herself from a low-hanging spider web, dozens of small, furry creatures with glowing red eyes flew down the hallway, nearly knocking Gloria off her feet. Nope, Gloria definitely couldn't shake the feeling that she didn't quite know what was coming.

Medieval Torture class was first. Sure enough, Mrs. Hastam lectured about odd and frightening weapons, and sure enough Mrs. Hastam didn't like Greta; she never called on Gloria when she raised her hand. Their homework, due at the end of the week (if at all), was to come up with a torture device of their own. They would be graded on their creativity and efficacy. Gloria remembered that Greta had a D in Mrs. Hastam's class. She knew a D was bad, but she wasn't sure *how* bad. She decided she'd do her sister a solid and really try to knock this project out of the park. A little bonus for Greta when they switched back at the end of the week.

In Banned Books class, they broke into small groups and read ghost stories aloud. Gloria was paired with two Moon Twins who kept picking their noses and putting boogers in between the pages of the book, another who doodled drawings of what seemed to be ghosts with giant teeth all over their legs and arms, and another girl who lay down on the floor and immediately fell asleep. Since none of them seemed interested in following the instructions, Gloria read all the stories to the group. The exercise reminded Gloria of public speaking; she liked having an audience, even if they weren't particularly paying attention. She did all the voices differently and then changed the ending for one, just to see if anyone was paying attention (they weren't). Nobody told her to stick to the script. She just did her thing.

Sure, the subjects in Moon School were infinitely more interesting than what Gloria was used to, but that wasn't the only thing that stood out. All the rules in Moon School seemed like suggestions. She almost felt as though she weren't in school at all. Classrooms were filled with random tables of different shapes and sizes. Sometimes there weren't enough tables, so Moon Twins sat on the ground, which seemed to bother no one. Kids interrupted one another nonstop and none of the classroom materials were organized or color coordinated. It was borderline chaos.

But a thrilling kind of chaos.

As the day progressed, Gloria started to wonder what on earth Greta had been complaining about this whole time. It was basically impossible to get in trouble, all the classes were super interesting, and they didn't have to sit in desks. Seemed like a major win to Gloria. And nobody had picked on her yet. Sure, nobody had really talked to her, either, but that wasn't the worst thing. There was just so much to take in.

Eventually, the school day was over and it was time for BLASTketball practice. Gloria hadn't been in the gym for more than three seconds before she started sneezing. So. Much. Dust. While Gloria put on her pads (*so* many pads—how was she supposed to move around in all that?), she looked out the window at the rain that slammed against the windowpanes. It really did rain *all* day long in Moon School. But something about the rain made her feel energized and daring. It also promised bigger puddles, which were irresistible to jump in.

"Hey, Sun Twin," a voice said from behind her. Gloria's stomach dropped. She'd been caught already! What gave her away? Her lack of skills when it came to eating with her hands? Or was it that she'd followed instructions too carefully during class? At one point she'd asked if she was allowed to go to the bathroom . . . had *that* been a dead giveaway? Gloria turned around slowly to meet her fate.

The girl standing before her had to be the infamous Lola. And it turned out the infamous Lola looked just like Gloria's best friend from Sun School, Lana. "Look, she responds to Sun Twin now!"

The girls behind Lola exploded with laughter. Gloria felt a ball of fury begin to build in the pit of her stomach. How *dare* Lola call her a Sun Twin. She *was* a Sun Twin, and it still made her mad.

"I came up with a new move today." Lola stood facing Gloria square on, hands on her hips. "I'm going to try it out on you first. It's called The Slicer."

Gloria took this opportunity to size up the girls standing behind Lola. Her crew; it had to be. One girl had red glasses that reminded Gloria of fire. Fire Glasses mimicked the way Lola stood with her hand on her cocked hip. Another girl viciously bit into a candy bar. Gloria remembered the third; she was the one who had grabbed Gloria's ankles earlier. She still had the most bizarre bangs.

But Gloria recognized the fourth. That was Mitten's Moon Twin. Was she really with them? It was hard to tell. She sat on the ground, a little bit off to the side, whispering to something she held in her hands.

It was a snake. Sharkbite. Yup, Mitten's Moon Twin had a *snake* named *Sharkbite*.

Moon School was bonkers.

"You think you can stop me?" Lola taunted. Fire glasses snickered behind her.

Gloria took a step closer to Lola. "You think you can stop *me*?"

Admittedly, it was not one of Gloria's best comebacks. But she had to say something, and it was the first thing that spilled out.

Lola gave her a funny look. "I guess we'll just have to see." She laughed and turned back toward her friends.

But Gloria remained confident. She brought with her a secret weapon—a secret Sun School weapon was the way she thought about it. No Moon Twin would ever see it coming.

Gloria leaned over and pretended to stretch her hamstrings while she waited for practice to start. Because there was an extra-heavy thunderstorm raging outside, all the other gym class activities had been moved indoors for the afternoon. At the far end of the room, Gloria watched a Moon Twin shoot a flaming arrow into a bull's-eye. Next to the flaming archery area, another group of Moon Twins took turns throwing large knives at the wall. Boy, Greta had really picked the wrong activity. Why would you play dumb ol' basket—or, rather, BLASTketball when you could play with fire and sharp objects?

"Alright, you cretins, time to get started," a hoarse voice called. Gloria looked up to see a woman with an eye patch waddling toward her. Everything about her—the voice, her leathery skin, the tracksuit that just looked plain itchy— reminded Gloria of sandpaper.

That must be Coach Sliver, thought Gloria, remembering the horror stories Greta had told her.

"Forget warming up. We're going to scrimmage all week. I'm going to use every moment as an evaluation. Anything you say or do can and will be held against you."

"How about you don't let the blast go off this time, okay?" Lola sneered as she walked past Gloria to the other end of the court. "Can you manage that?"

Gloria took a deep breath. This was intense. She was starting to understand what her sister had been complaining about. Gloria ran over the game plan in her head: Play along long enough to get the lay of the land, then go in with her secret weapon. *I got this*, she thought to herself, hopping in place to dispel the building nervous energy.

Sliver divided everyone into two teams—first team versus second team, she called it. Gloria was on the second team with Sierra (the snake girl), Rox (Fire Glasses), and the two nose-pickers from Banned Books class (Gloria didn't know their names). The scrimmage began, and Gloria did her best to follow along.

Nosepicker One and Nosepicker Two were real bruisers; they didn't miss a chance to get involved in every play. One seemed to prefer pulling shirts, while Two was all about the elbow to the gut. Sierra tended to lurk off to the side, constantly checking on Snakebite, who she kept inside her shirt pocket.

Greta had never mentioned that BLASTketball was the most confusing game ever. Gloria didn't understand how pulling someone's hair helped you win. Coach Sliver insisted they do something called Dashes to Ashes. Of course, Gloria didn't know what that was. It didn't take long for Chopper to knock her down and steal the ball. Coach Sliver yelled at her about giving away the turnover. Gloria soon realized it didn't matter *how* she did it—she just had to win.

Gloria let herself fall victim to hair pulls, shoves, and a few trips for several minutes. The more she watched, the more she was sure: Foul play was just plain inefficient. Her team, though generally the more aggressive, had fallen behind by ten points. It was go time.

Gloria dribbled the ball down the court. Lola, who'd been guarding her the entire game, got into a shoving match that was brewing under the basket. The candy bar girl, Tashi, now with a lollipop in her mouth, approached. She also chewed on a giant wad of bubblegum. That's when Gloria saw her chance.

Gloria knew there was no way she'd get past Tashi without getting gum in her hair (Tashi's move of choice). Most of the other players were preoccupied with the shoving match. Someone had Chopper's long braid in their hands. Lola was trying to pry that girl's hands off Chopper's braid with her teeth.

Gloria took one more dribble and looked to her left. Sierra stood just inside the three-point line all alone. Gloria dribbled again, and made her move.

"Sierra! Pass!" Gloria called, tossing the BLASTketball her way.

Sierra looked up just as the ball sailed past her and out of bounds.

Coach Sliver blew her whistle.

"What was THAT?!" Coach Sliver screeched.

"Not again," Nosepicker One moaned, rolling her eyes.

"Greta, you always ruin everything," Number Two added.

Coach Sliver stood in front of Gloria now. "Explain yourself, Garcia!" she thundered.

"Well," Gloria began, taking a deep breath. She would not let herself be intimidated. "Since this is technically a team sport and all, I thought a pass might—"

"A *team* sport?" Coach Sliver boomed. "Where did you get the impression you were to engage in any teamwork?"

Gloria shrugged.

"I know you didn't learn that from me. What have you been up to?"

"Um, nothing, Coach Sliver," Gloria squeaked.

"Are you *sure* about that?" Coach Sliver squinted her one available eye at Gloria as if she were out of focus.

Did Coach Sliver know? Impossible. Right? Was that pass too obvious? Was that too much to try on day one?

Coach Sliver took another step toward Gloria, then another, and then another. By now she was so close, Gloria could see the flecks of gray food stuck in her yellow teeth, and she could smell the coach's putrid peanut-butter breath.

Gloria started to sweat. She reached for her necklace to make sure her Moon Charm was still there. It was. But Coach Sliver still stared at her, her nostrils trembling and flaring, but her one eye remaining steady.

She knows. She has to know. Will she go easy on me if I just confess? Honesty was always described as the best policy in Sun School. (Of course, nobody ever broke the rules in Sun School, so it didn't come up much.) Maybe honesty was the way to go here, too?

Coach Sliver's eyebrows twitched now. Gloria couldn't take it anymore. She was about to open her mouth to speak when Coach Sliver's face broke into a sinister smile.

"Do you all see what I did there?" Coach Sliver said, addressing the group.

Lola shouted out, "Intimidation!"

"Very good, Lola. Intimidation is correct!"

Gloria let out a sigh of relief. Yup, that was some effective intimidation on Coach Sliver's part, but she hadn't broken Gloria. Not yet.

"Try to incorporate that into your game, Garcia. Let's go!" With that, Coach Sliver blew her whistle.

Gloria jogged to get back on defense. While Lola ran to get the ball, Sierra tapped Gloria on the shoulder.

"What's a pass?" Sierra whispered. Luckily, Coach Sliver's back was to them.

What's a pass? Gloria thought. How could she explain a *pass*? It was like explaining why the sky was blue; why peanut butter tasted like worm guts; why the sun rose in the morning and set at night. It just *was*. A pass was just a pass.

"It's . . . dumb," Gloria lied. "Forget about it." She didn't want to risk Coach Sliver overhearing her.

Gloria tried not to let BLASTketball practice get her down. She hadn't dared pass again, but in her efforts to avoid getting pushed or tugged on, she'd let the ball expire not one, not two, but *three* times. She'd been told by an enraged Coach Sliver that that was a Moon School record. Gloria's team lost 24 to 2. Apparently the second string always lost, but this was Gloria's first time being part of an athletic defeat. Yup, it would have felt better to win. Much, much better.

But Gloria reminded herself to think on the bright side. Yet another Sun School doctrine she usually ignored that, surprisingly, was coming in handy. It was only day one. She had plenty of time to make her mark. She couldn't let it bother her too much. Plus, it was dinnertime and Gloria was starving.

The dinner offerings at the mess hall were, well, bizarre. There were four long tables that reminded Gloria of the wooden tables of the Sun School dining hall. But these were much darker, and they didn't look to be made of wood. One table had three giant bowls of spaghetti noodles. Another had three giant bowls of pudding. The third table had large platters of meat doused in brown gravy. In what appeared to be a trash can sat a large pile of eggs. It was unclear if they'd been cooked.

It didn't seem like any of those items went together, but what did Gloria know? Avoiding the mystery eggs, she filled up three heaping plates; one with spaghetti, another with pudding, and the third with what turned out to be meatloaf (though what kind of meat, she hadn't a clue). She may have been in Moon School, but there was no way she was going to let all that food mix together. Some Sun School eating habits made too much sense to kick.

Gloria walked out into the seating area. When she passed Tashi, now with a neon-green lollipop in her mouth, the girl eyed her and muttered, "Multiple plates, huh? Interesting strategy."

Strategy? Gloria wondered, proceeding to the first available spot. If some Sun Twin logic rubbed off on these maniacs that easily, maybe getting the BLASTketball girls to follow her lead would be doable after all.

"Hi," Gloria said to the three girls as she approached the table. She didn't recognize them from class. They must have been a year or two younger. "May I sit here?"

They paused their chatter and looked at her with confused expressions.

"You don't have to ask," one said.

"Okay, thanks!"

Another looked at her with disgust. "You don't have to thank us, either."

Gloria took a seat. "Right, sorry. I mean, okay."

The girls sat in silence for a moment.

"Don't you just love pudding for dinner?" Gloria said cheerfully. Maybe a little *too* cheerfully. Oops. The three girls rolled their eyes, turned toward one another, and continued to talk among themselves.

Rude, Gloria thought. She was just trying to make conversation, but whatever.

Gloria noticed that several bright-red and bright-yellow squeeze bottles sat on every table. Ketchup and mustard. Again, interesting choices to go with spaghetti and pudding, but again, what did Gloria know? She squirted some ketchup onto her plate and dipped her finger in. She hadn't had any ketchup in years and couldn't remember if she liked it. Ew, way too sweet. Gloria didn't see any napkins on the table or anywhere in eyesight, so she took the liberty of wiping her finger on her shorts. Nobody stopped her. Nobody even batted an eye. So she dipped another finger in the ketchup and wiped it on her shirt. Just because she could.

As far as modes of consumption went, Spaghetti proved to be an extremely versatile food. Gloria tried slurping it up, one noodle at a time (super fun). She tried stuffing as many noodles into her mouth as she could at once (less fun). Then she noticed that when she dropped a noodle, it stuck to the side of her chair.

As Gloria continued to play with her food, she noticed that all the Moon Twins kept going back for seconds before they had finished their first helpings. Gloria's Sun instincts nagged at her. *How wasteful*, she thought.

Lola was the one to start it a few minutes later. Gloria had nearly finished dinner when Lola stood up on the table next to her and began to stomp her feet.

"What time is it?"

The Moon Twins didn't answer Lola's call, but they did begin to stomp their feet in rhythm.

"I said, what time is it?"

The stomps got louder. This was exciting, but Gloria was a bit confused. There was a clock on the wall clearly indicating it was three-thirty a.m. Dinnertime. Why did Lola keep repeating a question with such an obvious answer?

"What TIME is it?" Lola bellowed again.

The Moon Twins finally answered in unison. "Countdown!"

As if on cue, every Moon Twin in the dining hall stood up.

"Ten! . . . Nine! . . . Eight! . . ." As the numbers decreased, the volume increased. When they got to *five*, most everyone was either stomping their feet or drumming on the tables. *What is going on?* Gloria wondered. There sure were a lot of countdowns at Moon School. Greta had told her about the BLAST clock, but not this. This countdown seemed more exciting than menacing. Gloria stood up and joined the other students. She needed to fit in, both for her sake and Greta's, after all.

"Three! . . . Two! . . . ONE!" Gloria looked around. Now what?

"FOOD FIGHT!" All Moon Twins yelled at the top of their lungs.

Handfuls of noodles flew every which way. Globs of pudding soared through the air. A slab of dripping meatloaf smacked down right in front of Gloria, landing in the meager remains of her chocolate pudding. Bats dipped down from the ceiling, spooked by all the noise, and made the scene even more chaotic.

Now everything made sense. The menu, the second helpings. This had all been planned.

A glob of pudding hit the back of Gloria's neck. She spun around and saw Lola already winding up again with a handful of spaghetti. Before Lola could get her again, Gloria hurled the piece of meatloaf that had been lobbed at her toward Lola. It nailed her smack in the forehead.

"Ha-ha!" Gloria screamed, throwing her arms in the air. Triumph!

Lola looked at her with shock and rage in her eyes.

"It's on!" Lola shouted. The rest of her table turned their attention toward Gloria and fired. In no time, Gloria was covered head to toe with layers of spaghetti, pudding, and condiments. As Lola threw slices of meatloaf, Rox and Chopper double-teamed by squirting bottles of ketchup and mustard in Gloria's face. Tashi fastballed an egg that smashed into her chest.

Yup, the eggs were raw. And rotten.

Gloria was practically drowning in food. It was Lola, Rox, Chopper, and Tashi versus Gloria, and Gloria was definitely losing. How could she compete? It was four against one.

Gloria wiped a blob of pudding away from her eyes. Lola seemed to have given up on her for now; she was facing the opposite direction and throwing meatloaf at the Nosepickers.

That's when Gloria had an idea. She looked at the condiment bottles scattered on the table in front of her and grabbed a ketchup with her right hand. She stifled her instinct to let out a scream and charge forward. Instead, she snuck quietly on tiptoe, carefully concealing the red bottle behind her back. Lola stood on top of the table, her back still to Gloria.

Gloria jumped up onto the table and tapped her on the shoulder.

"Truce?" she asked when Lola turned around, in her sweetest, sunniest voice. Before Lola could answer, Gloria opened her left arm wide, pulling Lola close and into a big bear hug.

"What are you—?"

"Just hug it out," Gloria said, somewhat teasingly. While she had Lola in her grasp, she moved quickly. She hugged Lola with her left arm as she raised her right, ketchup bottle still in hand. *This one's for Greta,* she thought. Quickly, she pointed the nozzle down the back of Lola's shirt and squeezed as hard as she could.

"Aaaah!" Lola screamed.

"Sneak attack!" Gloria clutched her a little tighter, making sure Lola could feel the cold, slimy ketchup.

Lola pushed away, looking at Gloria with total shock, fury, and something else Gloria couldn't put a finger on. Then Lola smooshed a juicy piece of meatloaf all over Gloria's face.

Gloria jumped down from the table and tossed the meatloaf aside. She'd made her move, and she was happy to retreat. Plus, it looked like it was still raining. Might as well run outside and get a free shower. The smell of pudding, ketchup, mustard, and gravy was becoming a bit too much.

Before Gloria left, she noticed Sierra under Lola's table, cradling her snake and feeding it a piece of spaghetti.

Yup, it was still raining. Pouring, actually. Gloria stood on the path that linked the dining hall to Moon Dorm, held out her arms, and let the rain wash away the food that clung to her hair, neck, face, and clothes. After most of the pudding and ketchup was washed off, Gloria ran across the field and toward the edge of the woods. She had to let Greta know all about her first day as a Moon Twin.

Gloria wanted to tell Greta about the sneak ketchup attack on Lola for sure, but she also had some questions that needed answering ASAP. What was with Sierra and that snake? Did she ever notice that Coach Sliver smelled like peanut butter? Any advice on food-fighting strategies? But mostly, Moon School wasn't that bad at all . . . should she tell Greta that part, too?

Once she arrived, the mixture of food all over her body had been thoroughly replaced by mud. Gloria felt fantastic knowing that when she returned to Moon Dorm, nobody would notice or care that she was filthy.

Under the top-hat rock was a folded-up note waiting for her, written on the back of one of Lana's famous checklists. The familiarity of her friend's handwriting made her smile. Gloria felt like she had been away from Sun School for far more than almost twenty-four hours.

Gloria had been so anxious to get to the note she was sure awaited her, she'd forgotten to bring paper and pen. She dug in her pockets on the off chance there was something to write with.

All she found was a spaghetti noodle. Well, a noodle was better than nothing.

She also wanted to tell Greta that she was okay, and that she hoped Greta was, too. She hoped that Greta could determine all of that from a noodle. Gloria lifted the top-hat rock and arranged the single strand of spaghetti into a loopy heart. It wasn't much, but it would have to do for now.

Gloria skipped back across the field to Moon Dorm, jumping in every puddle she came across. The rain had finally eased up, leaving a dense fog and a soupy ground. She didn't have much time; daylight was fast approaching. As she neared the path leading to the dorm entrance, she saw the biggest puddle yet. The harder she jumped, the bigger the splash, and she wanted the biggest splash possible to end the day. Right before she reached the puddle, though, she saw something that stopped her in her tracks.

There, between stones, grew a single, but unmistakable, yellow tulip. Where had that come from? Gloria frantically looked around. Had anyone else seen it? When had it sprouted?

Gloria snatched the flower from the ground and smooshed it into her pocket. She looked down at the ground; it was as if it had never been there. Good. Yellow tulips didn't belong in Moon School.

Gloria scampered down the steps to the cellar. She had the sudden urge to jump on her bed. So, she did.

CHAPTER TEN

GRETA

"Can you *please* pass me another nail?" Lana asked.

With her foot still on the ladder, Greta searched through the toolbox on the table next to her. It was filled with wrenches, screwdrivers, and small pieces of hardware. Greta found a nail and handed it to Lana, who stood on the third rung of the ladder, hammering the finishing touches into the flower-arranging booth. "Here you go."

"Thanks!" Lana expertly (and carefully) began to hammer the nail into the plywood.

Greta, along with the rest of the Sun Twins, had spent the entire morning out on the big field, working on Gemini Academy Fair.

It was Sunday. In Moon School, Sundays were days off. Granted, Greta usually spent them alone, counting down the minutes until Monday, when she would finally have somewhere to be again, but at least she got to lounge around as much as she wanted to and sleep in. Today, Sun Twins were once again awakened at dawn to begin their building. Nobody seemed to mind. The truth was that Greta was happy to hang out with her friends and prep for the fair, too. It was a beautiful day: warm, and not a cloud in the sky. A breeze tickled Greta's cheek every time she thought she might be getting hot.

Something was bothering her, though.

That noodle. All Gloria had left her was a *noodle*? A noodle, Glo, really? She had to be kidding. What kind of note was *that*? Greta didn't need to be a Moon Twin rocket scientist to know that her sister had survived her first Moon Twin food fight. Duh. But Greta wanted details! How was she handling Lola? Didn't she agree that Coach Sliver was just the *worst*? Did she suspect anyone was onto them? Details, Glo, details!

All the Sun Twins were really good at basic construction. They spent every spring break building houses for those in need, apparently. By early summer, when the fair rolled around, assembling the booths, tents, and any other Gemini Academy Fair infrastructure was a cinch.

Greta had nearly broken her hand trying to hammer, so she'd been demoted to spotter while Lana stood on a short ladder and nailed two pieces of plywood together. Daisy and Aisha worked together on the opposite side of the booth, adding final reinforcements to the counter. Mitten was on the ground next to them, curled into a somewhat impossible-looking position, working on the lettering for the banner: *Flower Arranging! Come One, Come All!* She hummed a little while she painted. A large basket filled with yellow streamers sat nearby.

When Greta had gotten Gloria's note—ahem, *noodle*—that morning, she'd been so annoyed, she didn't write anything back. She didn't have much more to say at that point (she'd survived another excellent night's sleep in Sun Twin paradise, but that was about it). At least Gloria hadn't forgotten. That was a plus.

"Alright, I think this is good," Lana said, eyeing her work. "Nice and stable. Aisha, Daisy—how are you doing over there?"

"Thumbs up," Aisha said. Daisy mimicked her, giving an actual thumbs-up sign.

Greta stepped back to get a better look at the booth. It was pretty amazing. She couldn't believe that they had built it in just one morning. Well, not *her*. She didn't really feel like she had helped at all. Greta didn't like that feeling—that feeling of being on the outside reminded her of Moon School.

Greta gazed at the small rectangular structure and thought about what she might add. Or not add . . .

"We could leave a few booths without the streamer decorations," Greta suggested.

Lana giggled. "Very funny, Glo. What's with you and the crazy ideas recently?"

"I'm serious. The variety might be interesting."

"Hmmm," Lana said, rolling out the construction blueprints in front of her. "Well, all the booths are supposed to be the same. The plans call for streamers on all of them." Lana gestured toward a few of the other booths that had popped up around the field, built that morning by other Sun Twins, of course.

"Variety could be cool," Mitten said, her eyes still on her banner. Greta watched the way her paintbrush swooped as she drew a loopy cursive *L*.

"Yeah, but it's not in the instructions." Aisha pointed to the plans in Lana's hand.

"If the instructions say, *add lots of yellow streamers to all booths*, we should definitely add lots of yellow streamers to *all* booths," Daisy confirmed.

"Yeah, but think of it this way: If we leave some booths without streamers, then other booths can have *extra* streamers." The more she thought about it, the more she wanted to see some booths without excessive streamer decor. "Plus, not all the Moon Twin activities need to take place in a booth with yellow streamers."

"Since when are you thinking about Moon Twin activities?" Aisha asked.

"I think it's a bad idea," Daisy said.

"I think it's a not-so-bad idea," Mitten said.

"I don't know." Lana looked around nervously. Headmistress Solis was on the other end of the field. Greta watched her high-five a group of Sun Twins who'd just finished erecting another flower arranging booth. "Headmistress Solis would definitely notice and we might get in trouble."

That made Greta laugh. "The point is for everyone to notice. We're talking about *decorations* here. Anyway, it's such a small change. Why would that get us in trouble?"

"It's just not in the plans," Lana repeated. "You know that."

"And it's kind of a Moon-y idea," Aisha added, under her breath.

"You all, we need to stick to the plans so we stay on schedule. We can't get behind schedule!" Daisy began the early stages of hyperventilation. Aisha helped her find her way to a seated position on the ground.

"I bet people would come to our booth first if we had extra streamers," Mitten said. She'd moved on to the *O*. Greta noticed the *O* was more of an oval than a perfect circle. *What a great* O, she thought.

The idea of their booth being a special attraction made Greta excited. More than ever now, she wanted everyone at the fair to come to their flower arranging booth first.

"What does it matter if people come to this one first? There's going to—"

Lana couldn't finish her thought because suddenly a flying creature swooped down from the sky and into their booth. The size of a small bird, the animal flapped around and around, as if it were trapped. As if it were trying to create as much chaos as possible.

Lana shrieked and threw the plans in the air. Aisha covered

her head and took a step back, tripping over the tool bench and landing on top of Daisy. Mitten stayed on the ground and tucked her knees to her chest, somehow making herself even smaller. Greta held on to the ladder to steady herself during all the confusion.

Just as suddenly as the animal had appeared, it flew off behind the school building, vanishing completely.

Greta had spent long enough in Moon School that she could recognize those glowing red eyes and those leathery wings anywhere.

That was a bat.

In no time, Headmistress Solis had come over to see what all the commotion was about.

"It was the weirdest thing," Aisha said. "It just flew down out of nowhere."

They all stood on their feet, huddled around the booth.

"I've never seen an animal like that before," Daisy said, visibly shaken.

"Was it a bird?" Lana asked.

"That doesn't look like any bird I've ever seen," Mitten said.

Greta held her tongue.

"Children, children, it's alright! That was nothing other than a butterfly," Headmistress Solis insisted.

"A butterfly?" Lana asked. "I thought butterflies were pretty colors, like orange and blue and yellow."

"And pink," Daisy said. "I've seen a pink butterfly." She nodded vigorously as Aisha patted her back.

"Yes, a butterfly!" Headmistress Solis affirmed. Was it just Greta, or did Headmistress Solis sound more forceful this time? "In fact, the Tiger Longwing butterfly is very rare. This special visit is a certain sign of good luck and nothing more!"

A *sign*. The word stuck in Greta's head.

But Headmistress Solis's words seemed to soothe everyone. "Keep up the great work!" she said as she turned and walked away to observe the progress of the other booths. A scent of peanut butter lingered in the air after her departure.

"Okeydokey, where were we?" Lana said.

"Uh-oh."

Lana, Daisy, Aisha, and Greta turned toward Mitten, who was standing in front of the banner. A large splotch of green paint splashed across it, obscuring half her lettering. "The can must have spilled when that butterfly thing was flying around."

"The green paint was for the booth!" Aisha cried. "We haven't gotten to the booth painting stage yet! Why was the can even open?"

"I just wanted to add some green to the letters." Mitten looked ashamed. Greta felt bad for her.

"But that wasn't the plan!"

"I thought it would be nice," Mitten whispered, as if to herself, her voice shaking a bit.

"What's going on?" Daisy cried. "This day is *so* weird!"

Greta waited for Lana to jump in, but she just stared at the spilled paint.

"This is a disaster," Aisha said.

This was simply too much theatrics for Greta to handle. "This is . . . most certainly . . . *not* a disaster. We can spread the green paint over the whole banner, and then use the pink paint over it for the lettering." The girls stared at Greta, unsure. "I know it's not in the plans. But sometimes things just don't go according to plan!" The other girls listened on. "Thankfully, this problem has a solution. Think of it like making—" what was the expression again? "Lemons out of lemonade."

Mitten giggled. "You mean turning lemons into lemonade?"

"Right. That."

"I love lemonade!" Daisy exclaimed.

Lana gave Greta a nudge and smiled. "Way to save the day. Thanks, Glo."

Greta smiled back and did everything she could to forget about the bat. She had saved the day; she had done something right.

For a moment, Greta almost forgot about the bat. Almost. It was just a harmless bat, after all. It had probably lost its way. That's all it was. The bat had been lost.

Luckily, everyone seemed to lose interest in the butterfly-bat quickly once they started painting. Aisha and Daisy (forever joined at the hip, it seemed) worked with Mitten to turn the spilled green paint into a dynamic plant. Lana and Greta got to work painting the booth with the pink paint that had initially been reserved for the banner. At one point, Greta noticed Headmistress Solis staring at them from across the field. Greta waved. The Headmistress took a sip of tea and swallowed before she waved back.

"Glo, you're getting a sunburn," Lana said, touching Greta's shoulder with an index finger. Greta noticed that her skin had turned a shade of brown magenta that she'd never seen before. "Did you forget to put on sunscreen today?" Of course Greta had forgotten to put on sunscreen. In fact, she had totally forgotten about sunburns entirely. "You should put on a jacket before it gets worse," Lana suggested.

"Okay, I'll go grab one." Greta turned to go. "And thanks." She smiled. This was what friends were for, huh?

Greta skipped back toward the Sun Dorms, satisfied about her paint solution, oddly delighted to be sunburnt, her heart swelling with a feeling she couldn't determine, but for once, she felt like she belonged.

When she got back to Sun Dorm, she saw that the muddy spot she'd noticed outside the entrance was now a puddle. Greta could see it before she even got to the stone path. It was almost too big to jump over. Greta remembered the bat and got a sickly feeling in her stomach. She looked around quickly to make sure she was alone. Then, as fast as her arms would move, she dug up the nearby earth and mixed it in the puddle. She worked quickly, and her arms burned as much as her crisped shoulders, but she didn't stop until the puddle was completely gone. She stamped her feet on the ground to even it out. It was like it had never been there.

Greta hurried up the stairs to retrieve her jacket. She didn't want her friends to wonder what had taken her so long.

The puddle and the bat were too wonky for Greta to ignore. That night, just after Greta was sure the Sun Twins had fallen asleep, she snuck out to the top-hat rock. She had to leave Gloria another note.

It was really the bat that left Greta feeling the most uneasy. Why had a bat flown through the field during the day? And why had Headmistress Solis called the bat a butterfly? (Did she really not know those were two different animals?) And, perhaps most important, why was there a bat flying loose during Sun School? Greta had a funny feeling—a funny feeling that she didn't like one bit.

Greta didn't want to spend too much time where she wasn't supposed to be, but leaving a note for Gloria, that was worth the risk.

The fog was starting to come in. Pretty soon the sun would

be too far below the horizon to shine any light, the clouds would build, the rain would fall, and Moon School would begin. Greta scribbled quickly on the scrap paper she had brought with her.

Glo—

A bat flew into us while we were building the fair booths today. A bat! Bats are not supposed to be here! Could that have been a sign of some sort? Is anything strange happening in Moon School? You don't think we had anything to do with this . . . do you? Let me know ASAP!

Love, G

Greta looked around quickly, tucked the note under the rock, and scampered through the fog back to Sun Dorm. Both sneakers were caked with mud by the time she made it inside.

CHAPTER ELEVEN
GLORIA

On her second day of Moon School, Gloria did not wake up of her own accord.

"Get up, Ketchup."

"Ketchup? Where? Gross? No." When Gloria opened her eyes, her view of the ceiling was obscured by Lola's face.

"That's what I'm calling you now." Well, it was better than Sun Twin. *Not that Sun Twin is bad*, Gloria reminded herself. There was nothing wrong with a Sun Twin, unless you were in Moon School; then it was definitely bad, although the more she thought about it, she didn't totally see why . . .

Lola's raspy voice interrupted her spiraling thoughts. "Ground is lava. Come on."

It took a moment to realize Lola was not issuing a warning, but rather an invitation. The ground was not *literally* lava; this was just a game. A game Gloria loved.

Lola sprang up, jumping from bed to bed until she made it to the door. Gloria got up and followed her, attempting to avoid the legs of sleeping Moon Twins as she bounced from bed to bed.

"Hey!" the sleeping Moon Twins cried as they were suddenly

awoken. It didn't matter that it was rude—this was Moon School, after all. If anything, it was encouraged.

"Puddles don't count as lava," Lola clarified once they were outside.

Good thing, thought Gloria. There were a lot of puddles outside and not a lot else.

Gloria noticed that Gemini Academy Fair setup was in the works on the Great Lawn. She thought of her sister; she hoped the planning was going alright. She felt a slight twinge of regret as she noticed the framework for a booth of some sort. Gloria didn't miss fair planning, but she loved the build-out. Hammering nails into wood was one of her great joys in life. Nothing like building a structure to make you feel productive and accomplished.

"Neither do rocks," Gloria added, forcing her attention back to the present.

"Duh," Lola said as she jumped from a small puddle to a bigger puddle to a rock. Thunder rumbled overhead.

The duo jumped from rock to rock, bush to bush (bushes didn't count, either), and from puddle to puddle, until they reached the main castle. As it was Sunday, their day off from class, the halls were empty.

Gloria watched Lola swing from rusty iron lighting sconces and climb up the crumbling brick walls. At first, Gloria shadowed her, but then soon surpassed her.

"Follow me," Lola urged. "I know a secret."

Gloria trailed Lola into a utility closet with an orange door-knob, through a small metal door at the very back of the utility closet, and then through an even smaller door with another orange doorknob that led to a narrow hallway. By this point, it seemed Lola had forgotten about the game entirely. And the fact that it was nearly pitch-black.

"How can you see where you're going?" Gloria asked.

"Don't need to. Muscle memory." Lola was not the best tour guide.

"Where are we?" Gloria made her way by listening for Lola's footsteps and keeping a hand on the wall, which felt to be made of a cool, damp clay.

"It's a secret passage, obviously."

"Obviously," Gloria echoed. Her eyes were starting to adjust to the dark. There wasn't much to see; the hallways were bare and empty. Nope, not much to see, but it was certainly cool to be . . . wherever they were. Gloria got the distinct impression that not even most Moon Twins—Lola's friends included—knew about this.

The passageway narrowed, and just as Gloria was about to be officially too claustrophobic to proceed, they turned a corner. Dead end.

"Okay, so I guess we go back now?" Gloria offered.

"Not yet."

Lola stepped closer to the dead-end wall, and Gloria followed her. Then, she saw the door. It was mustard yellow, and it was locked.

"I've been trying to open this door forever. It leads to Sliver's office, you know."

"I didn't know." Gloria shook her head.

"Well, now you do. She shares an office with the Sun School principal."

"How on earth do you know that?" Gloria asked.

"Just do. I know lots of secrets about this place." For some reason, Gloria believed her. Lola added, "Don't tell anyone or I'll convince everyone you're a Sun Twin. Again."

Gloria almost choked on her spit.

"JK. Maybe." Lola tugged on the door handle. A surprisingly sturdy padlock made a thudding sound. "Locked, locked, locked. You don't have a wrench on you, do you? I heard that's the best way to pick a padlock."

"Uh, no. Didn't bring my toolbox with me," Gloria said sarcastically.

"Didn't think so."

Gloria faked a sneeze. "I can't breathe in here. Let's go back out to the hallways. I want to swing from those lighting things again."

"Bossy, bossy, bossy," Lola said as she followed Gloria out the way they came.

"You know, you'd probably be better at BLASTketball if you used more of that arm strength," Lola admitted after Gloria completed an especially long-distance swing from one wall sconce to another.

Gloria landed right behind Lola, in front of the door to Mrs. Hastam's classroom. Moon School was completely empty except for Gloria and Lola. It was kind of creepy, actually. But also kind of cool. More cool than creepy. It seemed like they were trespassing, which Gloria knew to be wrong. But it was also harmless. And fun. *Harmless, fun trespassing*, Gloria assured herself.

"Hey, look! Mrs. Hastam left the door to her classroom open!" Lola said. "She *never* leaves it open."

The girls crept into the dark classroom.

Lola went straight to Mrs. Hastam's desk and started rummaging through her drawers. "I know she keeps those chocolate-covered grasshoppers in here somewhere," she mumbled.

Gloria stood in the doorway, looking around. She had expected the room to look different somehow . . . like, mysterious. But it wasn't. It was the same, just empty and a little darker.

Just then, Gloria noticed something moving outside the window. She took a step closer to see if the movement was something more than precipitation.

"Domino!" Gloria shrieked.

The chipmunk perched on the ledge outside the window. As Gloria approached, she realized he must have been hiding out from the rain. He looked cold. And lost.

"Hey, buddy," she whispered, tapping on the windowpane ever so lightly.

Domino looked at her, and Gloria could have sworn he recognized her.

That's when it hit her: Mrs. Hastam's room was also Ms. Heart's art room. Gloria took her eyes off the chipmunk and looked around to make sure. Everything was different and rearranged, but it was definitely the same room. The classroom was the same place off the hallway, now that Gloria thought about it, and the windows looked out on the same oak tree.

"What on earth is *that* thing?" Lola demanded, pointing a shaky finger at Domino.

"Oh, just a little chipmunk."

"A what?"

Lola sidled up to Gloria and looked out the window. As Lola leaned forward, her Moon Charm clinked against the glass. "Ugh, this charm thing is so annoying. I hate having something around my neck all the time." Lola moved the Moon Charm to the back of her chain so it no longer dangled in front of her. "A chip-chunk, you said?"

"A chipMU—" Gloria suddenly caught her tongue. Lola didn't know about chipmunks. They didn't have chipmunks in Moon School, did they? "I mean, it's a . . ." Gloria had to think quick. ". . . a walking bat."

"Huh?"

"Yup, a rare species."

"Sounds like you're making that up."

"No way," Gloria bluffed. "You can read about them."

"Pfft. Like I read," Lola said walking away, already on to the next entertainment. "Let's go to the dining hall. All those tables and chairs will be perfect for a lava obstacle course."

Gloria pressed her forehead against the glass. She wanted one last look at Domino and a wave goodbye. Did chipmunks know how to wave goodbye? It was strange, but Gloria missed Domino.

"Greta—I mean, Ketchup—come on!" Lola insisted.

"Okeydokey." Gloria sighed. She gave up on Domino and turned around.

Lola stood in the doorway, stock-still, staring at her. "What did you say?"

"Um . . . okeydokey?"

Lola continued to stare at her curiously. "Where did you get that?"

"It's just a thing to say." Granted, a very Sun Twin thing to say, Gloria realized.

"That reminds me of someone." Suddenly Lola's face was soft and her eyes focused on something that was not there. She looked so much like Lana.

"Who?"

Lola blinked, and her expression hardened. "Butt out," she snapped. "None of your business."

Lola's words were like daggers. *Ouch*, Gloria thought, taking a step back and bumping into a chair. "You're a lot less fun when you're mean, you know," she said. It just slipped out.

Lola's eyes danced, but she didn't say anything right away. She took a few steps closer to Gloria. "Well, *you're* a lot more fun when you fight back."

The girls stared at each other for a few more seconds before Lola's scowl burst into a big, toothy smile. Gloria smiled back, and then Lola laughed, and then they were both laughing and laughing and laughing. Gloria laughed until her stomach hurt, until she saw tears welling in the corners of Lola's brown eyes. Before the moment ended—because Gloria didn't want the moment to end, just to extend—she grabbed Lola's hand.

"C'mon, race you to the mess hall. The ground is temporarily not lava. Let's go!"

"Okeydokey," Lola said between giggles as she followed Gloria out the door.

Nope, turned out Lola wasn't all that bad after all. Gloria wouldn't call her nice, exactly, but she was certainly more fun than mean after a few rousing hours of playing "the ground is lava." Maybe nice and mean weren't the only things that mattered. Lola was fun, and on an especially rainy Moon School Sunday, that's exactly what Gloria wanted in a friend.

A friend! Gloria had made a friend, which meant that Greta would have a friend when they switched back. And not just any friend—Gloria had befriended Greta's enemy.

Well done, Glo, she congratulated herself.

Gloria and Lola played "the ground is lava" until they were too exhausted to move. When they got back to Moon Dorm, they fell asleep before any other Moon Twins, long before the rain started to clear and the sun began to rise.

CHAPTER TWELVE

GRETA

By Wednesday, it had been two days since Greta had heard from Gloria. Two days! At this point, she'd take a noodle, a hamburger—any food or token that showed that Gloria was alive and that she remembered the purpose of their switch in the first place!

At first Greta was worried. Her imagination threatened to get the best of her. Odds were Gloria had not been locked in the Moon School dungeon (the rumored cell deep underground), or taken hostage by Lola and her minions. But there was no way to know for sure. It was possible that Lola, Coach Sliver, or any of the other teachers had sniffed the Sun Twin on her and punished her by doing who knows what.

Or maybe she was sick. Gloria wasn't used to all that processed junk the Moon School mess hall served. Or what if she'd been stabbed in the eye during a food fight? Rox had very good aim. Maybe she pelted her with an egg, or Tashi whacked her with a lollipop, and Gloria was blind and in the hospital, never to return!

The more Greta thought about it, though, the less likely any of that seemed. Gloria was a fighter. She'd go down kicking and screaming—tactics that would probably only elevate her status in Moon School.

A far more upsetting thought occurred to Greta: What if Gloria was having so much fun, she'd forgotten all about her sister?

Get a grip, Greta, she thought to herself. *Eyes on the prize.* And in that moment, the prize was getting through Intro to Botany. Gloria was right; sitting at a desk all class *was* boring.

Ms. Joy walked down the aisles returning the quiz they'd taken the day before. Of course, Greta hadn't known any of the answers. She'd missed the entire unit on *How Sun Saves the World, Part II: Photosynthesis.* What did Greta know about the sun's impact on plant life? She'd spent the past seven years in the dark.

When Ms. Joy returned Greta's quiz, Greta had turned it over without looking at it. Yeah, yeah, Sun School didn't give out grades, but there was no way she wouldn't at least receive a scolding of some sort. By the end of the quiz, she'd been so stumped that, instead of answers, she'd just started drawing pictures. A sketch of a flower had to be less offensive than gibberish, she figured. Regardless, Greta wasn't in the mood for a rebuke to top off the foul mood she was already in.

"Yes!" Lana exclaimed when she got her quiz back.

"What is it?" Greta asked glumly.

"The sticker is a leaf today!"

Greta flipped over her page and, sure enough, on the top right corner was a bright green leaf with a smiley face drawn in pen underneath. Ms. Joy hadn't left any additional marks on the page.

"Lana, can I see yours for a sec?" Greta asked.

"Okeydokey." Lana handed over her quiz and turned to chat with Aisha about her ladybug sighting. Apparently, Aisha had spotted one on a flower outside the dorms on the way to breakfast that morning. Everyone was hoping it would be back when they returned after dinner.

Greta looked at the two quizzes side by side. Lana's page had completely different answers from Greta's. No doubt Lana's were the correct ones. Yet, they'd still gotten the same leaf sticker. That didn't make sense to Greta. Her answers were clearly wrong.

"Hey, Lana," Greta called. "Do you think it's funny that we get the same sticker even though we put down different answers?"

Greta showed Lana their quizzes.

Lana gave Greta a puzzled look. "I don't understand your question."

"You got the answers right."

"Yes."

"But I didn't," Greta emphasized.

"Okay."

"But we got the same sticker. The same reward."

"A leaf sticker."

"Right. Doesn't that . . . bother you?"

"Why would it bother me?"

Greta sighed. "You did a better job than me but we're getting rewarded the same way. Why do you even try if you know you're going to get a leaf sticker no matter what?" Greta was getting frustrated.

"Well, it's not always a leaf sticker. Sometimes it's a tree, or a bird. There was a turtle that one time, remember?"

"Huh? Oh . . . sure, I remember the turtle," Greta lied.

"So, what are you saying?" Lana asked. It seemed as if she wanted to understand, but how else could Greta explain it? She gave up.

"Oh, nothing. I like the leaf sticker, too," Greta said. "It's my favorite."

"Yeah!" Lana said with more enthusiasm than Greta had ever witnessed someone have about a sticker. "Favorite. Yes! It's my favorite, too!"

This whole bizarre exchange only brought up more questions to add to the list of things to ask Gloria about, but Greta couldn't because Gloria wasn't writing her back.

Ugh.

Greta was over it. Over it all. She slumped forward in her seat and leaned her forehead on her desk. All the chipper voices around her, the sunshine pouring in, the soft violin music playing over the PA system—none of it was helping. In fact, it was somehow just rubbing it in that Greta was grumpy even though she had no real good reason to be.

"Glo, are you okay?" Lana asked. Reluctantly, Greta picked up her head.

"Don't worry about it. I'm just in a bad mood."

"Oh," Lana answered, as if she had just been pricked by a pin. "Okay."

Then, a few minutes later, Lana tapped her on the shoulder. "What does a bad mood feel like? I don't remember."

Greta didn't care if she was being reckless. She stomped out to the rock at the edge of the woods while the rest of the Sun Twins ate lunch. It wasn't like anyone would catch her. Sun Twins never broke the rules, and to catch her, they'd have to break a rule themselves. She was safe.

Frustrated, Greta wrote a note to Gloria:

> Since you've forgotten about me, why don't we just switch for good?

She wasn't planning on leaving it—that would be so mean— but it felt good to write her feelings down, to get them out. Then Greta saw a corner of paper sticking out from under the top-hat chimney rock, so she lifted it just to check.

She unfolded the paper to find her own handwriting. It was the last note she'd left for Gloria. It was still there! Greta grabbed her old note and ripped it to shreds. In its place, she put the mean, mean note she'd just written, but never thought she would have reason to leave.

CHAPTER THIRTEEN

GLORIA

Gloria and Sierra walked side by side down the hallway on the way back to class. Sierra whispered to Sharkbite, who lay coiled in her palms.

When Gloria got up to go to the bathroom during Mrs. Hastam's class, she was surprised that Sierra came with her. It reminded Gloria of the buddy system, a practice from the early days of Sun School, but not something she could imagine young Moon Twins being taught. *Does Sierra want to be my friend?* Gloria wondered. Her optimism faded, though, when Sierra ignored all Gloria's attempts at small talk during the journey to the lavatory. Still, Sierra waited for Gloria to wash her hands before heading back to class.

Sierra, not unlike her Sun Twin, Mitten, interested Gloria.

"You look so handsome today, yes you do," Sierra cooed. Gloria hid a smile. Sharkbite had really grown on her. "Don't worry, your fangs will come in any day now." Sierra touched Sharkbite delicately on his nose.

"Sharkbite is so cute," Gloria said.

Sierra glared at her.

"I mean—vicious," Gloria corrected. "Even without the fangs. Totally threatening."

"Yeah, he's my little fighter," Sierra said, petting the snake's tiny head with her pinky finger.

Suddenly, Gloria and Sierra heard a shriek from around the corner, then howls of laughter. Before the snickers faded, a swarm of bats (called a colony, if Gloria remembered yesterday's Nocturnal Creatures lesson correctly) shot toward them. Their leathery wings slapped against Gloria's cheeks as they flew past.

"What's going on?!" Gloria asked, charging around the corner.

Sierra followed but said nothing.

They found a small group of Moon Twins standing around an open locker. They were younger—third grade, maybe. As Gloria got closer, she saw that three little Moon Twins surrounded an even littler Moon Twin. The littlest sat with her knees pulled to her chest, as if trying to dissolve into herself. The standing Moon Twins continued to laugh—no, cackle. The littlest Moon Twin buried her face in her knees. A single bat flew back and forth inside the locker, as if it were trapped and didn't know how to get out.

Immediately, Gloria wondered what all these little Moon Twins were doing in the hallways during fourth period, but she remembered that Moon Teachers didn't seem to care if you got up and walked around during class.

When the young Moon Twins noticed Gloria and Sierra

approaching, they turned and ran down the hall, pounding lockers and breaking up cobwebs as they went.

"Don't be such a baby, Ruby," one called.

"Baby Ruby's afraid of baby bats!" another chanted.

A moment later, they were gone, and only Ruby and the disoriented bat remained. Then, the lone bat made its great escape and zipped away down the hallway. The bat seemed to make a point of flapping close to Ruby's head when it passed. Ruby yelped when the creature's wings beat against the back of her neck.

Gloria took a step closer. "Are you okay?" she asked.

Ruby hiccupped.

"They just startled me, that's all," Ruby squeaked. Her lip trembled. "I'm not afraid of bats. I'm really not. It's my fault. They hide bats in my locker all the time. I should know better by now."

Ruby unfolded her body a bit and bent over to pick up her notebook and a glass jar that had spilled out of her backpack. A tiny orange lizard crouched in the corner of the jar.

The lizard was extremely small and extremely cute. Perhaps the lizard, too, was growing fangs.

"Don't tell anyone I got scared, okay?" Ruby shoved her belongings into her bag and stood up. She only came up to Gloria's elbow. "Please?"

Ruby scuttled away before Gloria was able to nod her head *yes*.

Gloria and Sierra were alone again, the halls dark, damp, and empty once more. Sierra hadn't said anything the whole time. But Gloria noticed that she no longer held Sharkbite in her palm. The small snake sat on her shoulder, coiled back like a spring, ready to attack.

It wasn't until they got back to Mrs. Hastam's classroom that Sharkbite relaxed back into Sierra's shirt pocket.

Fifteen minutes later, Gloria sat on the floor, coloring next to Sierra. Mrs. Hastam had given them the entire period to work on the illustrated portions of the "design your own torture weapon" assignment. Before the bathroom break, Gloria had drawn her Traumatic Tickle Machine in pencil and was filling in the drawing with color.

Gloria didn't want to make a big deal of it, but she and Sierra were technically sharing markers: They'd been alternating the use of the red and the blue all class long. How unintentionally Sun School of them.

They hadn't spoken since they got back to class, but Gloria couldn't stop thinking about poor Ruby.

"Tell me, Sierra," Gloria asked, dropping the red crayon back on the ground. Sharkbite slithered out of Sierra's shirt pocket and onto her drawing. "What's the point of BLASTketball?"

"To push people down."

"No."

"To grab their shirts."

Gosh, Coach Sliver had really brainwashed these poor Moon Twins. Gloria took a breath and resisted the urge to answer her own question. "Nope."

"To trip them after the play is over?"

"No. That's not it."

"Is this a trick question?"

"No. Think about it."

"To somehow get the ball away from you before you cause the BLASTketball to explode and everyone laughs at you? Like what happens to you every time we play?"

Gloria ignored the dig. "No. I mean, kind of, but not totally. You're getting closer."

Sharkbite licked Sierra's finger while she thought. "I give up."

Patience must not have been a Moon School virtue.

"To score before the BLASTketball explodes," Gloria replied deliberately. "Right?"

"Oh, yeah."

"That's how you win, right?"

"Right. Winning. I love winning." Sierra picked up her snake. "Don't you love winning, Sharkbite?"

"Put Sharkbite down for a second," Gloria said. Sierra kissed the little snake on its lips (do snakes even *have* lips?) and tucked it gently back into her shirt pocket. Gloria looked Sierra in the eyes. "You want to win, right?"

"Yes. *Moon Twins always play to win*," Sierra recited rotely.

Gloria glanced around the room to make sure nobody could hear their conversation. "What if I told you there was a way to win without getting pushed over or intimidated?" Gloria couldn't tell if she was making it up or not, but Sierra seemed to fold inside herself a bit. Just like Ruby. "I know a better way to win than pushing people over and pulling their hair."

"No such thing," Sierra said, rubbing the back of her scalp.

"I promise, there is."

"But Coach Sliver says—"

"Forget what Coach Sliver says. She doesn't know *everything*, you know." Gloria rolled her eyes. For a Moon Twin, this Sierra was certainly obedient.

"What are you getting at?" Sierra picked up a new crayon and started a zigzag pattern across her paper. Gloria couldn't discern what torture method she was illustrating, but whatever it was, it sure had a lot of patterns. Looking at it for too long made her dizzy. Maybe that was the point.

"Meet me in the locker room five minutes before practice tomorrow. I'll tell you then." Gloria instructed.

"Tell me now."

"No, right before practice." Gloria didn't want to be rude, but she didn't know if she could totally trust her. Better not to give Sierra all the details in case she questioned Gloria's logic and backed out. Or worse, told everyone. "But I'll tell you this:

If you listen to me, our team will definitely win, and that nasty BLAST won't go off once."

"That BLAST really is so disgusting." Sierra considered Gloria's offer for another moment. "Okay. Deal, I guess."

"Remember, it's a secret." Upon hearing the word *secret*, Sierra seemed to perk up. "Top secret," Gloria emphasized.

"I love secrets," Sierra said devilishly. "Right, Sharkbite?"

Gloria rolled her eyes. "Right. Trust me. This will be the best sneak attack in BLASTketball history."

"You hear that, Sharkbite? We're going to be famous!"

Gloria hoped she could trust Sierra to follow through. She didn't really have a choice either way.

Gloria picked up a blue marker and returned her attention to her drawing: a person lying flat on their back with flowers under their armpits and feet. Hands were just as effective tickle instruments as flowers, but flowers were a million times easier to draw. If anyone asked, she'd say they were poisonous or something.

"Shoot, I messed up. Ugh, I wish there were such thing as a marker eraser." Gloria really hated coloring outside the lines.

Sierra glanced at Gloria's drawing. "You don't need an eraser."

"Yeah, right there, see?" Gloria pointed to the smudge that made one of the victim's legs longer than the other.

Sierra leaned over, took the blue marker out of Gloria's hand, and drew directly on her paper. Where there had been a wonky leg a moment ago, now there was an extra flower growing from the person's foot.

"I don't know why you do that," Sierra huffed.

"Do what?" Gloria stammered.

"Only color inside the lines."

Gloria stared down at her page and could no longer remember why staying in the lines had felt so essential.

On her way to dinner later, Gloria made a mental note to write an actual note to Greta. What she really wanted was to talk to her. She couldn't get Ruby out of her mind. Though she feared she already knew the answer, she hoped nothing like that had ever happened to Greta during her seven long years as a Moon Twin.

The dining hall was even more chaotic than usual. Was everyone food fighting already? Gloria tried to gear up for an immediate food fight, though after the long day, she was more in the mood to eat in peace than anything else.

As Gloria walked to pick up a tray, she saw Nosepicker Two dump a tray of perfectly good food into the garbage can and storm out.

"What's going on?" Gloria asked.

"Peas!" Nosepicker Two said, wild-eyed. "All peas!"

It clicked. On everyone's plates, instead of soggy fried food or dessert, there were bowls of peas. Green, nutritious peas.

This was not normal. Gloria had to let Greta know. If there were peas in Moon School, who knew what might be going on in Sun School? She scribbled a quick note on an unused napkin (also, since when did Moon School have napkins?) and ran outside.

When Gloria arrived at the top-hat chimney rock, she noticed a piece of paper sticking out from underneath. Greta must have left her a message! Gloria pulled it out.

Since you've forgotten about me, why don't we just switch for good?

Reading Greta's note felt like swallowing a pit. Gloria hadn't forgotten about Greta. Not really. Okay, maybe temporarily she'd gotten caught up in a food fight or two, and playing "the ground is lava" with Lola. And she was super distracted by Ruby, and then was hyper-focused on how to make her big BLASTketball plan work.

She'd forgotten.

Temporarily, but she'd still forgotten.

But still, *switch for good*? That didn't sit right with Gloria, either. It wasn't the *switch* that bothered her so much, though. It was the *for good*.

As she made her way back to Moon Dorm, Gloria saw Sierra crouched next to a puddle in the middle of the Great Lawn.

Had Sierra noticed she was out there? Doubtful, actually. As Gloria approached, she saw Sharkbite was swimming in the little pool of water. When Sierra was focused on Sharkbite, nothing else existed.

"Uh, hi," Gloria said solemnly.

"Hello."

"What are you doing?"

"Giving Sharkbite a bath. We're done now. He's nice and muddy and getting cold." Sierra picked up the snake and the girls walked toward the dorms together.

Sierra spotted the flowers first. On the path, right where Gloria had found one a few days prior. Except this time there were four.

"What are *those*?"

"I—uh—I'm not sure," Gloria stammered.

"Weird."

Gloria tried to laugh it off.

Not good, Gloria thought, as she went to pull them out of the ground. "So nobody else has to be exposed to this yellow plant monstrosity," Gloria explained.

"How considerate of you," said Sierra before she trudged her way into the dorms. Gloria didn't know if she meant that as a compliment or an insult.

The Moon Twins were still reeling from the pea dinner. If they saw this, who knew what might happen? She hated to pull perfectly good flowers, but Sierra was right; they didn't belong there. The yellow tulips didn't belong anywhere near Moon School.

Gloria followed Sierra inside, brought the flowers into the bathroom, and flushed them down the toilet. She comforted herself with the thought that perhaps they were poisonous.

CHAPTER FOURTEEN

GRETA

"Take the next few minutes to add the finishing touches to your embroidery patches," Ms. Heart said to the class with that singsong voice of hers. "Then, we'll use the rest of the period to stitch them all together. By the end of class, we'll have our community quilt ready to go!"

Greta pulled out Gloria's embroidery kit and considered the patch her sister had nearly completed. Then she looked at the model in the middle of the room—a small porcelain statue of an orange kitten. Greta looked back to the patch, then back at the cat. Then back to the patch, and back at the cat again.

The thread on Gloria's patch looked more like a bonfire than a cat. It would have been easy to fix. Just make the cat bigger to include all of Gloria's wayward stitches.

But then it would look like everyone else's.

This was Greta's embroidery patch now, and she didn't want it to look like everyone else's, so she decided to take some creative license. She prepared three different needles with thread—one yellow, one orange, and one black—put her head down, and got to work. Greta sewed quickly, but not carefully. That was okay; she had a lot to do and not much time to do it in. Greta and Mitten were the last two to finish.

With a minute left to spare, Greta tied the final piece of thread off and gazed at her artwork with pride. Now *that* was a cat. She looked over at Mitten's piece—what had taken her so long?—and gasped.

"Wow. Yours looks . . ." What *did* it look like? Greta racked her brain for the right words, but they didn't come.

Instead, Mitten spoke. Well, not spoke. She giggled, covering her mouth with one hand and pointing at Greta's piece with another. A mischievous, fun-loving giggle that Greta hadn't heard the likes of since she was last in Moon School. "Awesome," Mitten complimented.

The two girls brought their fabric squares to the center of the room, where Sun Twins were stitching their individual patches together to make one big quilt.

It didn't take long for everyone to notice.

"What . . . what did you *do*?" Aisha gasped. Daisy nearly fainted on the spot.

The Sun Twins gathered around to peer at Greta's square.

"How did—"

"The tail curves weird!"

"Crazy!"

"What are those dots?"

"Wild!"

"Why are its legs all different lengths?"

"Different!" Daisy exclaimed before she collapsed again into Aisha's arms.

"Why did you do that?" Aisha asked, struggling to keep Daisy upright.

"What's wrong?" Greta asked innocently. The class erupted with questions once again.

"Gloria, you didn't follow the instructions. The instructions were—"

"It doesn't match!"

"It sticks out like a sore thumb!"

"I think we should name it Checkers," Mitten suggested with a sly grin.

"It looks mean!"

"No way, Checkers is having fun. Look at the way he's chasing his tail."

"What will the people at the nursing home think?"

"Why would you make something purposefully bad?" Aisha demanded. The chatter stopped there. *Bad.* That was not a compliment. In fact, it was an insult. An insult in Sun School.

Greta felt a surge of hope.

Mitten spoke next. "Well, I love it. It's my favorite."

"Thank you," Greta peeped.

"I don't love it. I don't love it at all!" Aisha said.

"Aisha, apologize!" Lana hissed.

"She ruined our quilt. *She* should apologize!"

"It's okay, Lana," Greta said. "It's okay that she doesn't like it." And it was. In Moon School, nobody liked anything she did; she was used it this. "This was just the kitten I was in the mood to make."

"I think it's scary."

"We can't agree!"

That's the point, Greta thought.

"As Sun Class President, you should really be setting an example." Ms. Heart sounded more disappointed than angry.

"But I followed the rules of the assignment." *Rules of the assignment.* It sounded ridiculous to Greta when she said it out loud. Rules that led to order, rules that prevented food fights and name calling; those were good rules. Rules about how to make art . . . not so much. "We were supposed to sew a kitten onto our squares. I did that." Greta pointed to her square. "That's a kitten."

"It's true. A baby leopard is a type of baby cat. True, true, true." Mitten seemed taller all of a sudden, Greta noticed.

"It's not wrong. It's just different," Greta said.

Suddenly, there was a loud crash and the lights went out. Panicked Sun Twin cries filled the pitch black.

"What's going on?"

"Gloria, what did you *do*?!"

"Something ran over my foot!"

"Don't be dramatic, Daisy, just stay still!"

"It's just dark, no big deal!"

"It's not supposed to be dark—it's *daytime*!"

"Don't panic, children! Breathe! Remember our relaxation exercises!" Ms. Heart said over the prattle.

Greta felt the chaos around her in her body, but she remained still. She was no less concerned about the cause than anyone else in her class, but she was much less afraid of the dark.

Then, as suddenly as they had snapped off, the lights returned.

Ms. Heart clapped her hands twice. "Please, children, take your seats." The Sun Twins obeyed, happy to have an instruction to follow.

Ms. Heart ran to her desk and pulled out a book from a drawer. It was thick, leatherbound, and covered in dust. Clearly, this book had not been used very much. As Ms. Heart flipped through the pages frantically, Gloria read the bright-silver lettering on the spine: *A Guidebook: When Rules Are Broken*.

Sun Twins were so obedient, Ms. Heart literally had to read an instruction manual to remind herself how to discipline a student. Wow.

"Gloria Garcia," Ms. Heart said finally. She dropped the book onto her desk. It made a thump, and dust puffed up into the air. "Please go to Headmistress Solis's office at once."

Greta took one last look at the class before she walked out the door. Daisy sniffled. Aisha glared. Lana rubbed her cheeks and appeared completely disoriented. And Mitten had that mischievous smile on her face. Again. For a moment, her friends looked like they could fit in at Moon School just fine.

Greta was surprised to discover that Headmistress Solis's office was rather small, but very tall. Cramped, but not messy. Cluttered, but also, somehow, organized. Three of the walls contained floor-to-ceiling stacks of books. Their presence made the small office feel smaller, yet at the same time the books were all arranged by color, and that organization felt comforting. On the fourth side of the room, thick yellow curtains covered what Greta assumed were windows. Behind Headmistress Solis's desk was a large painting of a lake at night. The way the water shimmered and the way the stars above the lake seemed to dance was truly mesmerizing. On a shelf above the painting sat an ornate silver box the size of her head. It looked oddly familiar. Greta couldn't take her eyes off it.

Nope, this was not what Greta expected when she was sent to the Headmistress's office. It didn't feel like a part of Sun School, or a part of Moon School, either. Rather, this room seemed like the kind of space that existed nowhere else in the world.

None of this would have mattered if the office hadn't smelled like peanut butter. Gross. Greta breathed through her mouth.

"I asked you a question, Gloria." Headmistress Solis sat behind an oversize wooden desk, sipping a cup of tea. She slurped. Maybe that was the proper way to drink tea. Greta didn't know; she'd never had tea before in her life. Greta tore her eyes away from the silver box and focused on the Headmistress.

"I told you, Headmistress Solis, I *did* follow the instructions," Greta insisted.

Headmistress Solis sighed. "Are you acting out because you're anxious about the Gemini Academy Fair?"

"No," Greta answered right away. The moment after she spoke, Greta realized she didn't sound terribly convincing.

"You have a lot of responsibility as seventh-grade Sun Class President. I hope that pressure isn't getting to you."

Greta attempted to steady her voice. "No, Headmistress Solis, it's not."

"I've noticed that you've not quite been yourself recently," said the Headmistress. "Is there anything that you want to tell me?"

Greta gulped. *She knows. She must know.*

Headmistress Solis raised her eyebrows and tilted her head to the side. "You can tell me, Gloria. I'm here for you." Somehow, Headmistress Solis's invitation felt more like a threat.

Greta shivered. For a Sun School principal, Headmistress Solis sure was . . . creepy.

The Headmistress took another sip of tea. The sound reminded Greta of gravel. "You're not hiding anything, are you? Keeping a secret, perhaps?"

"No," Greta said quickly. "Sun Twins never keep secrets."

"No. Sun Twins don't keep secrets. But clearly something is bothering you. First, your outburst at the pep rally the other day, and now you're not following instructions in art class. That's not like you, not like you at all, Miss Garcia."

Greta looked at her lap. She couldn't tell where this was going.

Headmistress Solis continued. "What's next? Are you suddenly going to suggest we learn from our Moon Twins?" Headmistress Solis let out a shrill laugh that felt entirely too big and too loud for the small, tall room.

Greta pretended to chuckle along with her.

Then, Greta realized that two could play at this game. She was a Moon Twin, after all. Had she or had she not taken The Art of the Bluff? Never show your cards. Reveal nothing. Don't back down. Who knew that weird class would come in handy?

"Now that you mention it, there is *one* thing I'd like to get off my chest," Greta offered.

The Headmistress leaned in closer, reaching her hands across her desk. "Tell me, please."

"Something scared me, and I didn't know if I should say anything or not."

"Don't worry, dear, you're safe here."

"I . . . I saw a puddle. On Sunday, the day when that butterfly—what was it called again?"

Headmistress Solis looked confused for just a split second,

but she composed herself quickly. "Oh, yes, that butterfly. The rare Tiger Leatherwing."

"Right, the Tiger Leatherwing. It was right after that when I saw the puddle."

Headmistress Solis sighed and put down her teacup. "That's what I feared you might say. Yes, something has thrown our Sun equilibrium slightly out of balance."

Greta nodded.

"But don't worry about that one bit. I'm working to get to the bottom of it."

"I hope so. That puddle was really—" Greta paused, milking the moment. That silver box caught her eye again. Where had she seen that thing before? It was so distinct, yet she couldn't place it. "It was really unsettling. I think that's why I've been a little wonky recently."

Headmistress Solis's face softened. She sat back and smiled. All the energy in her body that had made her seem so intimidating a moment ago evaporated. "I understand. That puddle must have caused a real fright."

"I should have told you, or someone, earlier. It was too much to handle on my own. But I learned my lesson." Greta hung her head in mock shame. "Thank you for listening."

"Come here, dear. Let's hug it out."

Headmistress Solis opened her arms wide and Greta had no choice but to let herself be enveloped by a smothering hug.

Greta noticed the silver box again as Headmistress Solis pressed her into her shoulder.

Partly to release herself from the principal's grasp, and partly out of curiosity, Greta asked, "What's in that box?"

Headmistress Solis pulled back and raised an eyebrow. "The charms for the Induction Ceremony on Saturday, of course. How could you, of all people, forget?"

"Forget? I didn't forget. It's just a lot . . . *shinier* than I remembered."

Headmistress Solis took a step back and looked at Greta from head to toe, then back to head. "Make sure to get a good night's sleep tonight, dear. You look tired."

"Yes, Headmistress Solis." Greta turned to go.

"And don't forget to follow the rules. During art class, and always."

Relieved to be out of Headmistress Solis's office, Greta ran all the way to dinner. Sun School was a grand ol' time, but it felt nice to flex some of her Moon muscles. The Headmistress totally fell for her bluff about the puddle, and Greta was off the hook. Turned out all it took was several days in Sun School to prove how many Moon Twin skills she'd absorbed over the years.

But Greta's smile faded when she entered the cafeteria. Something wasn't right, but it took Greta a moment to figure out what was out of place. Then it clicked.

Nobody was eating. And nobody was talking. Every Sun Twin in the room stared at her plate in silence.

Greta approached her friends. "What's going on?" she whispered, not wanting to disrupt the silence, no matter how unsettling it was.

"Look," Lana answered.

"What? It's just fruit salad and pancakes, what's the big—"

"Pancakes with *syrup*!" Aisha scream-whispered. "Melon, pineapple, blueberries, grapes! Fruit *salad*! Why would they let all that fruit touch? It's horrifying."

"And dinner is not the time for breakfast food!" Daisy blurted. Of course, she looked pale.

"I bet it's good," Greta offered. In fact, she knew it was good. Breakfast at dinnertime was one of the main joys of Moon School. Wait—*of Moon School*. Uh-oh. Sun School. She was in Sun School.

Mitten, who'd taken to sitting with them for most meals since Sun Fair planning had begun, piercing a single blueberry with her fork. "I do love breakfast."

"Not for dinner! That's not right!" Daisy fussed.

"Glo, do you know anything about this?" Lana asked.

"N-n-o," Greta stammered. "Why would I know anything about this? I don't make the food or anything."

"You're right," Lana conceded. "I just thought maybe as Sun Class President . . ."

"You all, it's sweet!" Mitten said, wide-eyed. She didn't waste a minute before taking a bite of the pancake. Then another, and then another. "So. Good," she said, her mouth full.

"I'm not so sure we should be eating this. What if it poisons us?" Aisha whispered.

Before she could stop herself, Greta reached across the table and picked up one of Aisha's pancakes with her hands. She took a large, satisfying bite. Everyone stared at her while she chomped. Greta swallowed; everyone remained still.

Then, Lana took a nibble of hers, looking back and forth as she chewed. As if she were the authority, everyone waited for her response. "Wow...Yeah, they're right. This...this is good. *Really* good!"

Daisy took a bite with her eyes closed, chewing several times before spitting the pancake out into her napkin. "Way too sweet," she murmured, before carefully stabbing a single blueberry with a fork and popping it into her mouth.

"I'll take the rest of yours, then," Mitten said, picking up Daisy's remaining pancake with her fingers and dropping it onto her plate. "*Sharing is caring*, am I right?" she said with a wink.

Daisy trembled and chewed her blueberry.

Aisha, for once, didn't say anything. Instead, she cut a tiny piece of her remaining pancake and took a bite. Then she cut another piece, just as small, and ate that one, too. Then another, and then another. She didn't stop cutting and chewing tiny bits of pancake until her plate was empty.

Greta stole a glance at the other Sun Twins in the dining hall. Many Sun Twins sat staring at but not touching their food. Some poked at the pancakes with a fork, as if they were alien specimens. And others, like Daisy, extracted individual berries from their fruit salad. Amid the hesitant crowd, Greta saw, without a doubt, a handful of Sun Twins scarfing the food on their plates with gusto, simply enjoying breakfast for dinner.

The Sun Twins went to bed early that night. Everyone was exhausted, including Greta, though she hadn't fallen asleep yet.

Headmistress Solis was up to something, Greta just knew it. But even though the puddle wasn't the big secret Greta had been keeping, she felt slightly better that she had told someone about it. Even if that someone was a creepy old principal who smelled like peanut butter and slurped her tea and who was definitely (the more Greta thought about it) up to something. But up to what?

As she lay in bed looking up at the cathedral ceiling of Sun Dorm, it hit her. Tiger *Long*wing. Not *Leather*wing. Headmistress Solis had totally made it up.

Greta tossed and turned the rest of the night.

CHAPTER FIFTEEN
GLORIA

Practice started as usual. Coach Sliver divided the Moon Twins into their usual scrimmage teams, first string versus second string.

Gloria dribbled down the court and the play unfolded. Chopper flung her long braid at Rox to knock off her glasses. The Nosepickers furiously chased each other, holding out their index fingers, which were covered in boogers. Tashi elbowed anyone who encroached on her reign under the basket. Lola sidled up to Gloria. Sierra bounced on her feet to Gloria's left, just inside the three-point line. Nobody bothered her; they were too busy roughhousing,

"Let's go, Ketchup, no condiments to save you today." Lola gave Gloria a wink. Gloria half expected Lola to give her a break; they were friends now, after all. They'd stayed up late into the morning throwing jelly beans into each other's mouths from across Moon Dorm.

"It's never too late for a hair-pull! Don't forget to trip! Consider all your options!" Coach Sliver screamed from the sideline. She was already pacing around the court. The energy in the gym felt even more intense than usual. The fair was a day away. This was the last scrimmage before the annual game.

Gloria did her best to ignore the building chaos around her. If nothing else, foul play was distracting. Distracting and inefficient. And she was going to prove it.

Gloria stopped dribbling and looked to her right, locking eyes with Sierra. Sierra nodded. Lola took a menacing step toward her.

"Ooh, look who got herself stuck," Lola taunted. But Gloria remained calm.

She brought the BLASTketball to her chest and bounce-passed it right to Sierra's outstretched hands. Sierra caught it.

Lola swiveled her head to follow the ball. "What the—"

Gloria saw Coach Sliver raising the whistle to her mouth to stop the play. She was mad; her one good eye bulged out of its socket. But before she could interject, Sierra took one dribble and then shot a perfect, arching jump shot. Gloria watched the BLASTketball float through the air and—*swish!* Nothing but net.

The BLAST clock still had twenty seconds remaining.

"Lucky," Lola muttered under her breath. Gloria met Sierra's eyes and smiled. Sierra smiled back.

The next time Gloria got the ball, a few plays later, Lola didn't waste her time trash-talking; Lola charged at her full speed. The split second before Lola made impact, Gloria bounced the ball to Sierra again. Gloria watched from the ground, where she lay pinned under Lola's knee, as Sierra took another perfect jump shot. Another basket, and twenty-two seconds remaining on the clock.

The score was 8–12. Second string was losing by only four points.

Coach Sliver was unusually quiet. Suspiciously quiet. When Gloria looked toward the sidelines, she half expected the coach to be loading up a flaming arrow to shoot in Gloria's direction. Instead, she wrote furiously in a tiny notebook.

"That's not fair, you know!" Tashi complained after Sierra scored her second basket. "You're playing against the rules."

"Foul play forever!" Chopper chanted.

"Since when do we have to follow *rules*?" Gloria countered. "Why don't you stop complaining and try to stop us?"

Tashi and Chopper growled, but carried on.

"You better watch it, Greta," Tashi threatened.

Lola remained silent for once.

A few plays later, Gloria had the ball again. Her side was still down by a few points, but also closer than ever before to beating the first string. As Gloria dribbled up the court, Sierra darted across the paint to the other side of the court. *Nice improvisation*, Gloria thought. *Way to shake things up!*

Gloria drew in her defender, waiting until she had the right angle, and fired off a solid chest pass to Sierra. This time, though, the Moon Twins had caught on.

Instead of fighting among one another, Lola, Chopper, and Tashi all scrambled toward little Sierra, blocking the possibility of an open shot. Sierra yelped, and Gloria braced herself for the hits she knew Sierra was about to receive. Then, something amazing happened.

Sierra picked up her head, looked around, and saw Rox standing all alone at the free-throw line.

"Rox!" Sierra yelled, throwing the ball in her direction. Rox caught the ball and stared at it for a split second, as if wondering how the ball came to be in her hands. She blinked, and before any of the players could change direction once again to defend her, she shot the ball. Another basket!

"Yes!" Gloria cheered, jumping in the air. "Nice shot!"

Rox seemed stunned herself. "Thanks," she answered quietly.

Coach Sliver then blew her whistle so loud, Gloria was surprised the windows didn't shatter. The game paused.

Instead of getting onto the court and throwing a fit, Coach Sliver stood her ground on the sideline.

"I'm *disgusted*! You all don't know what you're doing," Coach Sliver insulted in a low but steady voice. "You don't know what you're doing at all!" She seemed to say that last sentence directly to Gloria.

Coach Sliver blew her whistle, longer and louder than ever before, turned on her heel, and walked right out the door.

The Moon Twins stood in shock for a moment.

"Whoa, what just happened?" Rox asked.

"She left," Sierra answered.

"Obviously," Tashi said, annoyed. "She must be mad. She

didn't even leave the other day when Greta let the ball blast three times."

Without Coach Sliver running the show, nobody seemed quite sure what to do. So, naturally, Gloria took charge.

"Well, we still have a scrimmage to finish, right? Looks like second string is only down by two points. I sense an epic comeback in the works," Gloria taunted.

"You all gotta stop doing that thing where you throw the ball back and forth. That's not fair," Chopper muttered.

"Why? You worried we're going to win all of a sudden?" Gloria challenged.

Everyone on the court looked at her funny. Gloria took it as a compliment.

Finally, Lola broke the silence. "Well, what are you waiting for? Let's go!"

The Moon Twins played and played. Second string continued to trail, but not by much. Soon, not only was Gloria and Sierra's team passing, but Lola's was, too. By the time the score was 24-22, Chopper had stopped using her braid as a weapon. When the score reached 34-30, the Nosepickers weren't shoving under the basket, and nobody had slammed to the ground after a late trip in minutes. Both sides played as if in a trance. The score climbed: 48-44, then 58-52, then 70-68. The Moon Twins played through dinner—they even played through bedtime. They never slowed and they never stopped. The BLASTketball never exploded, and Coach Sliver never came back.

CHAPTER SIXTEEN

GRETA

Greta awoke groggy and with a headache. Something was different. It was dark—not pitch-black, but dim. And a pattering on the roof and—holy moly! Was Greta back in Moon School?

She sat up in bed and looked frantically around the room. People were starting to stir, but, to her great relief, they were the right people. Sun Twins. Yes, there was Lana, Aisha, Daisy, and then Mitten at the far end of the room. Good.

But something still wasn't right.

Greta was so tired. She hadn't been this tired all week. Maybe everything was starting to get to her. She started to lie back down. Just ten more minutes and she'd get up.

Suddenly, what was unmistakably a crash of thunder shook the walls of the Sun Dorm. A flash of lightning electrified the room. Now Greta was up on her feet, ahead of the other Sun Twins who'd also been rudely awakened. She scrambled to the window, just to confirm what she already knew. It couldn't be. It couldn't—

But it was.

The sky was dark. It was raining. Flashes of white light illuminated the Great Lawn.

164

But that was impossible. It was morning, it was time for Sun School. It never rained or stormed during Sun School. Greta looked at the clock on the wall—seven fifteen a.m. Not only was it the beginning of the Sun Day, but it was late! Sun Twins normally awoke at seven a.m. sharp. Greta glanced at the clock to be sure. Now it read nine thirty. A flash of lightning momentarily illuminated the room with an unnatural glow. The hands on the clock began rotating out of control.

Uh-oh. This wasn't good.

Another crash of thunder. Behind her, Greta heard escalating wails and commotion. Daisy had certainly fainted. Greta continued to stare out the window; the Sun Twins would be okay. Probably. But the scene outside chilled her.

Puddles. Mud. The manicured lawn was starting to drown under pools of cloudy water. Thick black vines covered the bottom half of Gemini Academy. On the windowsill stood a line of birds, sheltering themselves from the rain. They, too, looked disoriented. A chipmunk scampered across the stone path below. And perhaps most tragic of all, the marigolds, tulips, and daffodils that lined the path and decorated the once perfect landscaping were wilted and drowning.

It looked like Moon School was eating Sun School alive.

"What on—" Lana had come up next to her. She pressed her fingertips to the glass as she looked outside. Then, she whispered in horror, "The fair."

Greta shifted her gaze to the Great Lawn. All the fair setup was exposed to the rain. Were plywood booths strong enough to survive these harsh elements? Actually, they were, it seemed.

"Our banners!" Aisha screamed. Greta turned around and watched as Daisy fainted again and all the Sun Twins stampeded to the window. "They're being destroyed!"

Aisha wasn't wrong. As the rain pelted down, the once beautiful loopy lettering that advertised flower arranging-stations, compliment circles, and refreshments had begun to drip and bleed, distorting the words altogether. The paint was neither waterproof nor water-resistant.

"They're going to be ruined!"

"What does water do to a banner?"

"It's not water—it's rain!"

"I hardly remember rain!"

"Rain *is* water!"

Over the clamor, one voice pierced through the air. It was Mitten. "We have to save them. Let's go!" Her rallying cry proved effective. Without changing from their pajamas, the Sun Twins rushed out the door.

Even when weathering their first storm, Sun Twins could organize and execute like a well-trained battalion. Within minutes, they had gathered all the banners and anything else that appeared perishable.

"Let's bring everything to the gym to dry!" Greta suggested. She hoped everyone could hear her. The wind was starting to pick up.

"Good idea," Lana shouted. Even in crises, a Sun Twin never missed an opportunity to compliment.

Off the Sun Twins went, arms full of waterlogged signs and soaked to the bone, sprinting full speed ahead to the gym. They splashed through puddles and trampled flowers, not stopping once until they were safe indoors.

CHAPTER SEVENTEEN

GLORIA

The Moon Twins sat in a line on the first row of the bleachers, the game temporarily paused for a water break. For the first time that scrimmage (or ever), second string had the lead, 90–88. Gloria was getting tired, but she wasn't going to slow down now. Her team had found their rhythm; if they kept it up they'd be up by ten points in no time at all, she just knew it. Gloria couldn't believe how well her passing plan had worked. Looking back, she'd considered it a long shot. But here they were; foul play was out and passing was in.

Gloria spotted Sierra at the water fountain. Gloria waved her over, patting the open spot next to her. She wanted to tell her how great she'd been playing, and to thank her for helping to start the passing trend.

Sierra saw Gloria, smiled, and started to trot over. Gloria noticed Sharkbite's absence. Was it just Gloria, or did Sierra look a little taller today?

"Look, I'll prove it," Gloria heard Chopper whisper to Tashi, a few seats down. Gloria, too, turned to watch.

The rest happened very quickly.

When Sierra ran by, Chopper stuck out her foot. Sierra went flying. When she landed, her elbows squeaked against the floor. Even before she pushed herself up, even before she looked behind her to figure out what happened, Sharkbite slithered out from under her shirt and coiled on top of her head. He looked just as disoriented as Sierra.

"See? I told you. She *always* has him. He's like her little protector or something," Chopper sneered.

Sierra pushed herself up to stand, then cradled Sharkbite in her hands.

"It's okay, Sharkey, you're okay." Sierra clambered away, past Gloria and the open seat, continuing to whisper to her reptilian friend.

That's when Gloria realized something.

Moon Twins didn't push and shove and trip and fight just to win. They did it to . . . Why did they do that? It was mean. Had anybody ever told them they didn't have to be mean?

"C'mon, let's go," Lola called, bouncing the BLASTketball at half-court. "First team: We got a game to win!"

Gloria was tired and disappointed, but she still wanted to compete.

Lola started with the ball. She dribbled straight down the court. Gloria stayed light on her feet, ready to defend. She heard the squeaks of sneakers on the court behind her, but her eyes remained on the ball. Lola bounced it right, left, right, left. Plenty of time on the BLAST clock. Gloria watched Lola scan the court, looking for a pass. No go. Instead, she faked to the left, then took a quick step to the right. The last thing

Gloria remembered thinking was, *Lola's even harder to stop without the foul play.* As Lola took a step past Gloria, preparing to drive straight to the basket, a stunning ray of sunshine shot through the windows, a light so bright, so sudden, and so penetrating that Lola lost her balance—and, momentarily, her vision—and toppled to the ground.

"Too. Bright." Lola cried, writhing on the ground.

Gloria rushed to her side. "Are you okay? What happened?"

Before Lola could answer, a clap of thunder shattered the windows. Somehow both sunshine *and* rain poured through.

Gloria felt a gust of wind; she turned around as the double gym doors blew open. Outside, she could see the hail pummeling down. And yet, sunlight simultaneously illuminated the other end of the gym through the glassless windows. There, in the doorway, stood a gaggle of Sun Twins, holding big pieces of soggy cloth, soaking wet.

Greta led the pack.

As if marking the occasion, the BLASTketball, which bounced lazily on the ground, rolled toward the door and stopped just in front of Greta's feet. It detonated. The smell of flowers filled the air.

And then things went completely berserk.

CHAPTER EIGHTEEN

GRETA

At the sight of their Moon Twins, some Sun Twins froze, some trembled, but all of them dropped the piece of the banner in their hands and screamed at the top of their lungs, in terror or shock, or both.

It never occurred to Greta that the Moon Twins would be in the gym. Weren't they supposed to be in bed by now? What time was it, again? Time, though, now felt irrelevant, as they stood across the gym from their Moon siblings.

And Gloria.

There she was, helping Lola up from the ground.

So it was true. Gloria had betrayed her.

Greta didn't have time to ponder. Chaos erupted.

CHAPTER NINETEEN
GLORIA

Gloria ran toward Greta, but a swarm of bats and butterflies engulfed her, knocking her off her feet. Gloria shielded her face to protect herself from the furious winged creatures. Then she felt a hand on her shoulder, then a hand in her hand.

It was Lola.

"Come on—I know a back way out."

Lola pulled Gloria up and they made their way to the back of the gym, where a small door appeared that Gloria had never before noticed. They went through the door, out of the gym, away from the Sun Twins—away from Greta.

CHAPTER TWENTY

GRETA

Wails filled the air. Once the bat and butterfly swarms cleared, Greta had to blink to get her bearings. It was as if the sight of their Moon Twins and the shifting weather was too much for anyone to handle. Half the Sun Twins turned to run back outside, but another gust of wind slammed the doors shut, threatening to trap them inside. Greta stood paralyzed, watching everything unfold around her.

The doors blew open again, and hordes of Moon Twins rushed to the exit behind her. Greta would risk being trampled, but she pushed forward against the crowd. Soon, she was alone in a dusty gym full of rainwater and a few random sneakers that must have fallen off various feet in the shuffle. But Gloria wasn't there. Greta spun around toward the exit, nearly slipping on a puddle of water, and went outside.

Things weren't much better out there. One second the sky was black and gray. Piles of hail gathered on the muddy, trodden grass. Thorny bushes grew at an alarming rate, as if their branches were tentacles. Bats whizzed through the air like they were on a mission to search and destroy. Then, a moment later, the sky magically cleared, sunlight filtered through a rainbow, and butterflies hovered over the drenched grass and mud. Marigolds and daffodils rocketed from the ground, sprouting inches in just a few seconds, overtaking weeds. Greta watched as the plants grew first to her knees, then to her waist, and then over her head. Just when Greta thought they wouldn't stop, the sky turned dark, thunder crashed, and rain flooded down. The flowers didn't vanish; instead, they began to wilt, as if they, too, were hiding from the deluge.

After several cycles of the back and forth, the disorienting weather pattern settled. The sky found a compromise: the slate-gray clouds were a little too transparent to be proper Moon clouds, and too, well, cloudy, for Sun School. The overgrown yellow flowers drooped, forming shelters or hiding places, depending on how you looked at it. Tufts of grass formed small islands within large puddles. Greta noticed that the Gemini Academy crest displayed neither a sun nor a moon; it was blank.

Sun Twins and Moon Twins buzzed around like bees. Greta watched, paralyzed. Nobody knew where to go or what to do. Chopper stormed out of a flower patch (apparently, she'd gotten tangled in a rapidly growing marigold stem) holding her nose and screaming, "It's worse than a BLASTketball!"

A trio of younger Moon Twins surrounded a lone Sun Twin. Ms. Heart, who'd just come running out of the gym herself, yelled out into the air, "Use your words, children!"

Mrs. Hastam chased Rox, who in turn chased her Sun Twin.

Aisha swatted a bat away that seemed intent on landing on her head. "Stupid Tiger Longwing, get away from me!"

This was not good. Greta never could have predicted this was what would happen when Sun and Moon Twins were together again. She and Gloria definitely had something to do with this; Greta was sure of it. She needed to find Gloria—and fast!

Greta scanned the landscape. On the near edge of the Great Lawn, several Sun Twins held hands in a circle and sang a lullaby. Daisy ran from her Moon Twin, who followed her, pitching handfuls of mud at her back. Sierra and Mitten stood in a puddle and observed each other curiously, as if the other were a precious alien.

Lana came up behind Greta. "This way," she said, grabbing Greta's hand and pulling her underneath a gigantic wilted daffodil.

Together, they hunkered down and watched the scene before them unfold.

By this point, Greta expected Headmistress Solis or Coach Sliver would have emerged, insisting that all the students fall into some sort of order, but they remained absent. The more Greta thought about it, the stranger that was. This was the craziest thing to happen in the history of Gemini Academy, and the principals were nowhere to be found.

Lana fiddled with her Sun Charm nervously. "Where *is* she?" she said under her breath.

"Who?"

Lana looked at Greta, wide-eyed. "Lola."

That was a good question. Greta still hadn't caught a glimpse of Gloria since they'd first emerged into the gym. Maybe Lola and Gloria were together. The thought of that stressed Greta out more than the pandemonium before her.

Greta took a closer look at the chaotic scene. It wasn't just Sun Twins and Moon Twins fighting. Between the clashes she noticed small moments of serenity that made the whole scenario even more strange. Some younger sisters, maybe they were seven or eight, hugged each other and laughed. Another pair of twins sat across from each other, talking quickly, catching up, as if they didn't know how long the moment together would last, making every precious second count. Yup, this was strange, but also hopeful.

"What's going to happen?" Lana asked.

"I don't know," Greta answered after a moment. "I really don't know."

CHAPTER TWENTY-ONE
GLORIA

The main castle was downright creepy, nothing like the last time Gloria and Lola had prowled through. Gloria would rather have been outside in the chaos that she could only imagine was unfolding.

Gemini Academy was clearly off-balance, and something about the quiet of the abandoned hallways made that fact all the more unsettling. Gloria followed Lola down the corridor, just as she had earlier in the week. Except now, the halls felt more threatening than if they had oozed real lava.

"This is wild," Lola said.

She was right.

One side of the hallway was covered in cobwebs and dripping candles. The other was lined with bright yellow walls and squeaky white floors. Gloria peeked into one classroom on her left. Sun desks were strewn about, toppled over. In the classroom to her right, Moon tables were arranged in straight rows, a chair placed at every seat.

As the girls progressed, the divide between worlds became less clear, less organized—almost as if things were shifting before their eyes.

C 177

"Let's get out of here," Gloria suggested. "It's worse than outside."

Instead of answering, Lola stopped short and held her finger to mouth. *Listen*, she mouthed.

Yup, those were voices, all right, and they were coming from inside Headmistress Solis's office. Gloria couldn't quite make out what was being said, but it sounded like arguing. It also sounded important.

Gloria motioned for Lola to follow her. They crept closer to the office door, concealing themselves behind a row of lockers. From that position, Gloria could hear perfectly.

Headmistress Solis and Coach Sliver were arguing. She'd never heard them together, Gloria realized. Their voices sounded strikingly similar.

"We should have been more careful."

"How?"

"I don't know, but we must have been able to prevent this somehow."

"How can it be our fault? This has never happened before!"

"Which two are responsible?"

"I have some ideas."

"How are we going to explain this? The new students arrive for induction tomorrow morning!"

"You're useless. Leave it to me."

Gloria could hear footsteps nearing the office door.

"We have to go!" Gloria whispered.

And with that, the two girls took off in a dead sprint in the opposite direction.

CHAPTER TWENTY-TWO

GRETA

Greta had been crouched in the flower patch for nearly ten minutes, and nothing seemed any closer to calming down. She was about to step out, brave the chaos, and look for her sister when Gloria and Lola emerged from around the castle, their eyes filled with worry. Before Greta got a sense of where they were headed or where they might have come from, Lana sprang up beside her.

"Lola!" she called.

Lola and Gloria slowed and turned their way. As Lana ran toward her, Lola's face seemed more panic-stricken than before. Lola ran back toward the gym, Lana close behind her. But they didn't keep Greta's attention for long.

Greta locked eyes with her sister. Without needing to say anything, they knew.

Greta followed her sister toward the woods, running as fast as her legs would carry her, heading straight for Lake Vetiti.

CHAPTER TWENTY-THREE

GLORIA

Gloria and Greta lay sprawled on their backs on the rocky shore of the lake, panting. The chilled stones pressed uncomfortably against her spine, but Gloria was too tired to care. She had never run so fast in her life. Her lungs were about to explode. She closed her eyes and worked to steady her breath. It was calmer, way out here by the lake. The fog was dense and the air felt wet and heavy, but it was quiet. Still. She felt as if she'd left the chaos of Gemini Academy behind. If she kept her eyes closed long enough, would it all just go away? Could this all be a fevered Sun Dream?

She smooshed her eyelids shut as tight as they could go and balled her hand into a fist.

Then she felt a sharp pinch on her arm.

"What the—"

"This is *your* fault!" Greta blurted.

"What are you talking about?"

"If you hadn't forgotten about me, if you had checked the top-hat chimney rock and read my note, you would have known!"

"Known what?"

"Known that weird things have been going on all week. We could have tried to fix it earlier. We could have—"

"What, Greta? We could have what?" Gloria demanded. "Switched back?"

The girls stared at each other in silence.

Gloria's heart felt like it was on fire. She had a feeling Greta's was equally torched.

"Everything is messed up," Greta said, softly.

"I know," Gloria agreed. "But it was going so well before all . . . before the weather got all weird and the flowers and peas."

"We got puddles and bats," Greta added.

"Yikes. The Sun Twins must have lost it."

"Yeah, sometimes they did. But sometimes they didn't," Greta said pensively.

"I'm sorry I forgot to check for your notes. But I didn't forget about you." Gloria felt her chest tighten as she spoke. "I didn't do this alone, Greta. We did this together."

Then, as sometimes happens when the utter truth is spoken aloud, Gloria and Greta started to cry. They held each other tight, and their charms clanked together.

"I'm sorry," Greta said. "I just want to fix this so badly."

"I know," Gloria whispered, holding her sister tight. "So do I. I'm sorry, too."

Several minutes later, the girls were pacing back and forth. Gloria kicked a large stone into the water. Greta picked up a handful of pebbles and flung them into the lake as far as she could, not bothering to skip any over the surface of the calm, flat water. Despite the chaos of the day, the surface of Lake Vetiti retained its signature shimmer.

"The Moon Twins learned how to pass!" Gloria exclaimed. Greta gave her twin a skeptical look. "Really! They were all doing it on their own. Which is an important first step. If only I had more time, then maybe they would realize all the foul play off the court isn't always necessary, either."

"I got sent to the principal's office," Greta admitted with a coy smirk.

"You did not." Before their switch, Gloria had tested quite a few Sun School rules, but she'd never come close to getting sent to speak with Headmistress Solis. Gloria was impressed.

"I did! For sewing a leopard cub for that quilt thing."

"Why? A leopard is still a type of cat," Gloria confirmed.

"That's what I said!"

The girls stopped pacing and giggled for a moment. It was a nice break from the chaos. They looked out at the water and sighed.

"I think we're in over our heads," Gloria admitted. "I hate to think it, but maybe our switch is causing more problems than it's solving."

"Aha!" The voice came from behind them. A second later, Lola exploded out of the woods and onto the shore. "I knew it!" Lola proclaimed.

"Lola, wait!" Lana said, breathless, popping out of the shrubbery, panting. "Why are you running so—whoa," she said, once she saw everyone.

The four stood looking at one another.

Gloria felt a tickle on her foot and looked down. A small green snake slithered by. Where there was Sharkbite, surely not far behind would be—

"Sharkbite! Slow down and come here!" Sierra scrambled onto the beach, finally catching the snake in her hands before the animal reached the water. "Oh. Hello," she finally greeted.

"Anybody else out there?" Gloria called, half-kidding.

They heard a rustling in the brush, and a moment later Mitten's head popped up from behind a bush. "Hi."

Things had just gone from bad . . . to worse.

CHAPTER TWENTY-FOUR

GRETA

"How did you know?" Greta asked. The six of them—three sets of twins—stood together at the shore of the lake.

"It was really that first food fight," said Lola. "Greta—the old Greta, or the original Greta, whatever—I'm not sure, this is confusing, but you know what I mean. *That* Greta," she said, pointing an accusatory finger at Greta, "would *never* have gone for the *ketchup-down-the-shirt* move. No way. Period."

Greta pivoted her toe between a few stones. She didn't know what ketchup move Lola referred to, but that didn't mean she couldn't have done *a* ketchup move. Greta was still a little on edge around Lola. The last time Greta had seen her, Lola had just thrown meatloaf at her face.

"Honestly, I've known you've been sneaking out at night for years," Lana confessed to Gloria. "After a while, I figured it was to meet with your Moon Twin. I was always a little jealous, actually."

"Really?" Lola said.

"Really."

"I wish I would have known." Lola looked . . . sad. "I'd have snuck out anytime." Yup, she looked very, very sad.

185

"What was it like living in Moon World?" Mitten asked. She knelt on the shore building a tower out of stones.

"It was fun," Gloria admitted. "Different. But not all bad like Sun School makes us think."

"Sun School was fun, too. It's super weird not getting grades, but everyone is a lot friendlier," Greta added. "And the food is better."

"No way!" Gloria said. "I'd take pudding and noodles over vegetables any day."

"Okay, so there *are* bad things about each," Greta said.

"But also good things about each, right?" Sierra asked. Sharkbite hung over Sierra's shoulder. He looked sleepy, like he was ready for a nap.

"Exactly," Gloria and Greta said at the same time.

"I'm not sure I want to go back to Sun School. I'm going to miss you guys," Gloria said softly, looking at Lola and Sierra.

"I'm going to miss you," Lana said to Greta. Greta felt her shoulders droop. Lana was the first friend she'd made in Sun School.

Then, Lola looked at Lana and smiled. Greta realized just how identical they looked.

Mitten picked up a pebble from the top of the tower she'd built and handed it to Sierra.

The six of them sat together in silence.

"It's so pretty out here," Mitten said, maybe to the group, maybe to herself. She added another rock to her tower. "These stones are so cool. They look kinda like our charms, the way they shimmer and all. I didn't even know this place existed."

"Well, it is forbidden," Lana said.

Lola reached up to give her sister a high five. "It's fun breaking the rules with you."

Lana blushed.

Suddenly, a voice boomed over the PA system.

"UNTIL ORDER IS RESTORED, SUN TWINS MUST REPORT TO SUN DORMS AND MOON TWINS MUST REPORT TO MOON DORMS. CAMPUS IS OFFICIALLY ON LOCKDOWN."

Everyone groaned.

"SUN TWINS." Headmistress Solis's voice echoed through the forest. "PLEASE HELP OUR COMMUNITY. HUG A FRIEND—"

Another voice interrupted the Headmistress's plea. It was Coach Sliver. "MOON TWINS, DON'T BE FOOLED BY A SUN TWIN WITH OPEN ARMS: HUGGERS ARE NOT YOUR FRIENDS."

"Maybe we should get back," Lana said. "Before we get in trouble."

"They think that's going to solve things?" Lola said, pulling a pebble out of her shoe. "Just locking us up in our separate dorms?"

The girls looked up at the sky. It was still gray. Gemini Academy remained in limbo.

Static played over the PA system. Another announcement. It was all Headmistress Solis this time.

"OUR INTEL HAS REVEALED THAT ONE PAIR OF TWINS IS RESPONSIBLE FOR THROWING OFF THE DELICATE EQUILIBRIUM OF THE SCHOOL. TURN YOURSELVES IN FOR THE BETTER OF GEMINI ACADEMY SO THAT ORDER MAY BE RESTORED."

"Do you really think your switch is why everything is so crazy right now?" Lana asked.

"What else could it be?" Gloria said.

Greta suddenly felt very powerful.

"You know," Mitten ventured. "I don't think everything that happened this week was all bad. Sure, the weather going back and forth is a little unpleasant and all, but now our fair banners have that cool green vine all over them. That wouldn't have happened if you two hadn't switched."

"And second-string never would have won that BLASTketball scrimmage if we hadn't learned how to pass," Sierra added.

"Just because we stopped while you were ahead doesn't mean you *won*," Lola insisted, her nostrils flaring a bit. "But we definitely scored more points than ever before. That counts for something," she continued after a moment, her tone softening. "Plus, the BLASTketball didn't go off once during the scrimmage."

"And, after all, a leopard is still a cat, right?" Lana admitted.

"Right," Gloria confirmed. "And coloring outside the lines isn't so bad after all." Gloria gently nudged Sierra's shoulder.

Greta nodded. "Yeah, a lot of good came this week. No doubt about it."

More static crackled overhead. Another announcement.

"IF THOSE RESPONSIBLE FOR THIS DISRUPTION DO NOT TURN THEMSELVES IN BY THE INDUCTION CEREMONY TOMORROW, FOR THE SAKE OF ORDER AND STABILITY, THE GEMINI ACADEMY FAIR WILL BE CANCELED."

"No! That is so unfair!" Lola screamed.

"How could they?!" Lana sobbed.

"It's all because of us!" Gloria howled, nearly in tears. "Why did I think we could get away with this?"

Nobody answered.

"We have to switch back." Gloria said. "Right, Greta? That's the only way to fix it, I think."

Greta didn't answer.

"Fix it how?" Mitten wondered aloud.

"So things will go back to normal?" Lana said. The words came out of her mouth like she was chewing something rotten.

"What do you think, Greta?" Gloria asked. "Should we switch back to save the fair?"

Again, Greta didn't say anything. She just held her charm and watched the lake's soft waves sway in and out. The water, like the stones, looked almost iridescent in this light. Was the lake always that color?

"I REPEAT," Coach Sliver's voice bellowed over the PA system, "REPORT TO YOUR DORMS IMMEDIATELY. CURFEW IS IN EFFECT IN T-MINUS FIVE . . ."

"We've got to go," Lana said, pulling at Lola's arm.

Lola tried to pull herself away, but Lana held on to her hand. It occurred to Greta that maybe Lana was the only one who wasn't afraid of Lola. Maybe that's why Lola was so mean when her twin wasn't around.

Sharkbite slithered off into the woods. Sierra ran after him. "See you all back there. Don't do anything stupid or fun without me! SHARKBITE!"

"Switch back or whatever. You guys got us into this mess; you all have to fix it," Lola said, turning to go.

"She's being rude, but she's right," Lana said sadly. "Switching back may be the only option."

She followed her sister into the woods.

Mitten stood, slipping a single stone into her pocket. She took a breath, as if she were about to speak, but no sound came out. Then she, too, disappeared into the woods.

Greta and Gloria were alone again.

"We've ruined things for everyone! We can't just not do anything!" Gloria cried, tears dripping down her cheeks.

"I'm not going back to Moon School," Greta said confidently.

"But will things stay this wonky forever, then?"

"I'm not going back to Sun School, either," Greta added, ignoring Gloria's question.

"What do you mean? Where are you going to go? We have to turn ourselves in! You heard her—they're going to cancel the fair because of us if we don't!"

"Maybe the fair isn't the most important thing. I don't know about you, but I'm not in the mood to celebrate anything Sun *or* Moon right now," Greta said. "If you think about it, what makes you a Sun Twin and me a Moon Twin, anyway? Just this stupid necklace?" Greta grabbed her charm.

Greta looked down at the Sun Charm that hung around her neck. It was just a stone. A pretty, shimmering stone, but still just a rock. A rock in the shape of a sun that had nothing to do with her, or her twin, or any other girls at Gemini Academy. "If only we could get rid of these," Greta said. "Like, all of them. Not just ours, but all the ones in the future."

"The Induction Ceremony is tomorrow," Gloria said glumly. "It's too late."

"If I could get my hands on that silver charm box, I'd take them and"—Greta looked around, as if deciding what she'd do—"I'd throw them in the lake. I don't care how much trouble I'd get in," Greta said bravely, before deflating a bit. "Ha. Yeah, right."

191

"Headmistress Solis probably keeps that thing under her pillow," Gloria muttered.

"If by under her pillow you mean in that strange office of hers," Greta said.

"Wait! It's in her office?" Gloria said, getting excited. "Are you sure?"

"Yeah, Glo, I was just there for the whole leopard incident, remember? It's right behind her desk under this weird painting. But it's not like we just can waltz right in and take it."

"I have an idea," Gloria whispered. "It's risky, but I think it could work. The only thing that stands between now and the Induction Ceremony is another Fraturday, right?"

"Yes."

"So let's make this one count."

CHAPTER TWENTY-FIVE

GLORIA & GRETA

Despite the campus lockdown, neither Gloria nor Greta had difficulty sneaking out of their dorms. After all, they were pros; they'd had seven long years of Fraturday practice. This Fraturday, though, they did not go back to the lake.

The sisters met at the entrance to the castle. On one side of the door, waist-high marigolds grew from a muddy patch. On the other, a lifeless daffodil floated in a cloudy puddle. Yup, things were still wonky.

Though they had much to catch up on, the sisters didn't chatter or even speak. They slipped into the building and moved swiftly down the dark, abandoned hallways. The wrench Greta had swiped from the Sun School toolbox weighed down her right pocket. It thudded against her leg, but it didn't make a sound. Not even the bats noticed their presence.

Gloria led Greta to the utility closet with the orange doorknob, and then through the small metal door at the very back. Through there, they ventured to the even smaller door with another orange doorknob. Once in the narrow passageway, she shut the last door behind them. The sisters paused to catch their breath.

"Are you sure we should go through with this?" Gloria asked.

"Do we even have a choice anymore?" Greta said. "We got this."

Gloria and Greta fumbled through the dark until they reached the final door: the door to the office. To their surprise, the giant padlock they were expecting was gone.

Gloria got a funny feeling in her stomach. This didn't seem right. Was it a trap? Before Gloria could voice her concern, Greta pushed the door open. Bright light flooded the passageway. To their horror, standing in front of them, blocking the threshold to the office, were Coach Sliver and Headmistress Solis, both staring down at them, as if they had been waiting for trespassers all along.

"You really thought you could get in here without us noticing? My goodness, what are you teaching in Moon School these days, Sliver? Certainly not the Art of Sabotage."

"Amateurs," Coach Sliver said, shaking her head.

Gloria and Greta sat in the office while Headmistress Solis and Coach Sliver hovered above them. They were too terrified and shocked to speak.

"I imagine you were looking for this?" Headmistress Solis taunted, picking up the charm box. "You were going to take it and dispose of the charms, thinking that would solve everything, weren't you?" She laughed and took a long, slurpy sip of tea. Even the tea smelled like peanut butter. "You fools!" she said with a dramatic flourish. The teacup fell to the ground and shattered. "There are plenty more charms where these came from!"

Coach Sliver interjected. "Solis, why don't you—?"

"We could go out to the lake right now and gather enough stones to make Sun Charms and Moon Charms for every twin girl from now until the end of time!"

"Solis, be quiet!"

But Headmistress Solis couldn't be silenced. She was on a roll. She, too, liked the sound of her own voice, it seemed.

"Ha-ha! One pathetic attempt at a heist won't stop us! We'll never run out—"

"Solis! I said shut up!" Coach Sliver thundered, pounding her fists on the desk. "This is precisely the opposite of what I teach in Interrogation 101. Never spill the beans to your prisoners!" Coach Sliver shook her head. "You've learned nothing running that Sun School of yours. Nothing!"

Greta and Gloria shifted uncomfortably in their chairs. Now they felt like they were listening to a conversation that was most definitely not about them. Yup, this conversation was rooted in something much bigger.

"Can I—?" Greta said timidly.

"SILENCE!" both principals boomed, united against the twins once again. Coach Sliver adjusted her eye patch and grinned menacingly. Headmistress Solis tucked a loose strand of hair into her head wrap.

"We won't be hearing another peep out of either of you until the Induction Ceremony," Coach Sliver promised.

Headmistress Solis cracked her knuckles and then took a long slurp of tea. "You two are going to restore order to Gemini Academy, whether you like it or not."

Gloria and Greta stood backstage. They held hands. Coach Sliver hovered behind them, gripping their ponytails tightly with each hand, assuring they couldn't escape. Headmistress Solis was in front, the silver charm box in her hands. A peculiar natural light from the large skylight overhead illuminated the room; the sky was still gray. Gemini Academy was still so out of whack that the time of day had become indistinguishable by the weather.

From where they stood, Gloria and Greta couldn't see the audience, only the two rows of inductees onstage. The young twins looked not so different from Gloria and Greta when, seven years prior, they had walked across the same stage and received their Sun and Moon assignments. Greta couldn't tell if the little ones looked more excited or more scared. Probably a little bit of both, if Gloria remembered correctly.

Most of them held hands, too. This made Gloria's and Greta's hearts heavy. From this day forth, they would rarely see their sisters again.

The auditorium buzzed with energy from the entire Gemini Academy student body. The Induction Ceremony was typically the most thrilling event of the year. That, paired with the absolute chaos of the past twenty-four hours and the following lockdown—well, the air in the auditorium was electric. It seemed everyone was alert but on edge.

Gloria and Greta had been taken straight to the auditorium from the principals' office. Fragments of Headmistress Solis's lecture still swirled in their heads: *The only way you'll ever feel like a Sun Twin again* and *Your Moon Twins will never forgive you.*

They knew what was coming. Kind of.

"On my cue," Headmistress Solis snarled before walking onstage. Her words sounded more like a threat than an instruction.

Coach Sliver jerked each ponytail. "Don't even *think* about trying anything clever."

The Headmistress walked onto the stage, an eruption of applause following her (well, at least from one half of the room). "Hello, Gemini Academy!" She greeted the crowd, then waited for the applause to die down. "Please welcome our new class of incoming students. Do give these new twins your warmest welcome."

The Sun Twins in the audience cheered and the Moon Twins in the audience booed, because, well, that's just what Sun Twins and Moon Twins did. Some of the inductees waved at the audience, others attempted their best glares, and some just held on tight to their sisters' hands.

Gloria and Greta didn't say or do anything.

"Before we get to the charm portion of our ceremony, I am afraid we must begin this occasion on a somber note. It's no secret that things have been, well, a little . . . strange . . . for the past day or so. With a heavy heart, I must tell you that two of your fellow students are responsible for the chaos and upheaval."

The audience went suddenly quiet. So quiet that Gloria and Greta both wondered if there were even people out there.

"These two twins who have betrayed you, and betrayed Gemini Academy as an institution, will now come forward, confess, and"—Headmistress Solis side-eyed Gloria and Greta—"apologize."

Before Greta or Gloria could take a step, Coach Sliver shoved them from behind. Together they stumbled onstage. It wasn't the graceful and dignified entrance they had hoped for.

A collective gasp resounded through the auditorium. Everyone in the audience started shouting out at once.

"The Garcia twins?"

"How could they?!"

"I always thought you were a perfect Sun Twin!"

"But she taught us how to pass! That was fun!"

"And she saved our flower booth that day, remember?"

"Moon Twins, Moon Twins, fight fight fight!"

Soon, everything jumbled together.

"Everyone, everyone—*SILENCE*!" Headmistress Solis barked into the microphone. "Give Miss Garcia and Miss Garcia your undivided attention."

The crowd quieted. Headmistress Solis gave the girls a final push toward the microphone and stepped back. Greta and Gloria stood center stage, together in the spotlight.

Gloria looked at Greta, and Greta looked at Gloria.

Gloria spoke first. "Hi."

"Hello," Greta added.

"I'm sorry if—" Gloria faltered. She didn't know if she could continue. She wasn't sorry. Not at all. She didn't know what she had to be sorry for. *I'm sorry that I pretended to be a Moon Twin.* That's what she was supposed to say, but she just couldn't do it. In fact, she couldn't say anything. The thrill she had once felt when speaking to a crowd—the excitement of anything being possible—was gone. Gloria wanted to tell the truth, but she was afraid.

It was a good thing she had her twin by her side. She gave her sister's hand a squeeze; Greta gave Gloria a squeeze back.

"What Gloria means—what we *both* mean—is that we're not sorry at all." Greta said defiantly. A shocked gasp spread through the sea of students before them. "We switched on purpose, and we'd do it again! What makes a Sun Twin all that different from a Moon Twin, anyway? Just this dumb charm?" Greta pulled the Sun Charm—Gloria's Sun Charm, that is—from her neck and held it for all to see. "This is just a rock on a necklace!"

The audience stared at the Garcia sisters in stunned silence. Gloria gripped Greta's hand, which was still slipped inside her own. She had a brave twin sister. And she wasn't going to make Greta be brave alone. Gloria took a big breath. Maybe the biggest breath she'd ever taken before. That was better. *It's now or never*, Gloria realized.

"I don't need a Sun Charm to be able to value teamwork and common courtesy," Gloria declared. "But I also should be allowed to color outside the lines and jump on my bed without a Moon Charm around my neck."

"Right! And the time I spent in Sun School showed me that compliments and predictability are awesome, but not without a little competition and variety thrown in. I shouldn't have had to trick everyone and switch places with my sister just to get a taste of Sun School," Greta added.

Some people in the audience started to shift uncomfortably, but there was no stopping the Garcia twins now. They were on a roll.

"Our point is," Gloria said, turning toward her sister, "you don't have to choose Sun School over Moon School."

"Or Moon School over Sun School," Greta confirmed. "You can love winning *and* teamwork!"

"Nobody is just one thing!" Gloria shouted.

That's when Greta realized she'd discovered what she'd been looking for all along: her *thing*. Perhaps Greta's *thing* was that she was more than just *one* thing. How had she ever thought she could be defined by just *one* attribute? She liked to compliment and compete, improvise and plan, follow most rules but also sneak out on Fraturday to meet her sister every once in a while. Greta Garcia was the sum of so many *things*, some known, and some undiscovered. Suddenly, Greta wasn't in a rush to figure them all out right away.

Gloria thought back to her first hours as an undercover Moon Twin. Years of practice looking on the bright side helped her cope when she screwed up during the BLASTketball scrimmage. Her Sun skills had aided her time and time again while in Moon School.

Greta glanced at Gloria again. They continued to hold hands. They were on the same page.

"We are better together!" they proclaimed in unison.

I have such a brave twin sister, Gloria thought.

I'm so lucky I'm not in this alone, Greta thought.

But their triumph was cut short. Before the audience could respond to their campaign, Coach Sliver rushed to the stage.

The audience sat in stunned silence. Coach Sliver pulled Greta in one direction, while Headmistress Solis tugged Gloria's arm in the other.

"That was *not* part of the plan!" Headmistress Solis said. Then, into the microphone, she bellowed, "The Induction Ceremony is over. New charms will be given in private. Report back to your dorms. Now!"

The audience started to rustle. This was unprecedented. The Induction Ceremony cut short? Charms in private? This was simply unheard of. It was—

201

"Wait!" a small voice called from the back of the auditorium. There, in the very back row on the Moon side of the audience, Mitten stood on her seat. "It's not just them."

"We switched, too!" Sierra yelled, also standing on her chair on the Sun side of the auditorium. She'd taken out her braids; her hair was now fashioned in two puffs atop her head, just like her sister.

"And maybe we did, too," Lola cried, jumping up onto the Sun side.

"We sure did!" Lana confirmed from the Moon side.

Not one to bow out of a disruption, Chopper jumped onto her seat. "I could have switched!"

"I could be a Sun Twin, too! Who knows?" Tashi called.

"Or maybe I switched, and I'm a Moon Twin!" Aisha yelled from the front row.

Never one to deprive her best friend of support, Daisy hopped up. "If Aisha and Lana and Gloria all switched, I would switch, too!"

The shouts continued to increase in volume and frequency.

"Maybe I've been switching places with my Sun Twin for years!"

"I never switched, but I always wanted to!"

"Same! I've wanted to check out Moon School ever since I got my Sun Charm!"

"I never wanted a charm in the first place!"

Then, as if all on cue, Sun Twins and Moon Twins together

did what they did best—they created organized chaos. A crew of twins in yellow outfits ran onstage to protect the increasingly panicked group of new inductees. A group of twins in midnight-blue shorts and T-shirts rushed the stage right behind them. Headmistress Solis tried to escape off to the right, clutching the silver charm box to her chest, and Coach Sliver lunged toward the wings on the left. But it was no use; they were surrounded.

"Get back, all of you! You don't know what you're doing!" Headmistress Solis screamed, backing away from an approaching line of sixth graders.

The twins were closing in. It wasn't going to end well for the principals.

Nobody noticed, but the weather was changing. As the twins swirled around the stage, hail beat down on the skylight above, only to shift to a sparkling blue sky a few seconds later. Hail to blue sky, dark to light, rain to sun.

Greta and Gloria watched their classmates run rampant around them. They had somehow gotten stuck on the inside of the circle with Headmistress Solis and Coach Sliver.

The circle continued to close, the two heads of Gemini Academy standing back to back in the center. Headmistress Solis attempted to reason with some Moon Twins on one side, while Coach Sliver faced the opposite direction and threatened a crowd of Sun Twins.

"You'll never get your hands on these!" Headmistress Solis

declared, spinning around to make a break for it in the opposite direction. Instead, she smacked into Coach Sliver, and the silver charm box flew into the air. The lid popped off and then—

A flash of lightning or a blinding ray of sunshine—nobody could be sure—shot down through the skylight. The strike was so bright that, for the second time in two days, everyone was blinded. A loud noise—the sound of shattering glass, or splintering wood, or both, echoed through the enormous space. Every twin felt a sudden chill—or was it a twinge of heat—right at the dip between their collarbones.

Gloria grabbed her sister's hand.

It took their eyes several blinks before the light had dimmed enough to see properly. Headmistress Solis and Coach Sliver lay sprawled in the center of the stage. The principals looked disheveled and dazed and frightened.

"Look, it's that walking bat!" Lola exclaimed.

Sure enough, Domino scurried out of a small hole in the floor and over to the principals. Domino approached Coach Sliver first, sniffing her hair, her forehead, then her eye patch. He paused and considered the entranced twins surrounding him; they truly were a captive audience. As if he'd been planning it all along, he used one little paw to pull off Coach Sliver's eye patch, then darted over to Headmistress Solis and tugged off her head wrap. Somehow, he managed to scuttle through the crowd, both items in his possession, vanishing into the wings as suddenly as he had appeared.

Without the head wrap to hide Headmistress Solis's birthmark, and the eye patch to conceal Coach Sliver's bright blue eye, it was undeniable that the two heads of Gemini Academy were nothing short of identical twins.

But that wasn't the only thing the crowd noticed.

Between the fallen principals, the silver box was broken in half, and beside the broken pieces was a mound of shimmering, pearly sand. Or dust. Nobody could be certain.

"Glo, look!" Greta raised a trembling finger toward her sister. The corners of her mouth twitched upward and her eyes flushed with happy tears.

Gloria didn't have to look down where Greta pointed to see, nor did she have to adjust her gaze to notice that in her periphery all the other twins onstage stood in shock, their fingers curling to enclose the charms that rested at their collarbones. There, clear as day, dark as night, hung new charms around everyone's necks: shimmering pearly discs, neither shaped like a blazing sun nor a crescent moon, but the form of the imperfect, irregular stones from which they were made.

ONE YEAR LATER . . .

Gloria added one last stroke of sky-blue paint to the canvas, then set her paintbrush down. She glanced out the window of Ms. Heart's classroom. It had been overcast that morning, but now, as sunset quickly approached, the sky was clear.

Behind her, Tashi and Rox giggled as they engaged in a paint battle. Tashi smeared a handful of yellow all in Rox's hair. Rox retaliated by dumping a can of purple over Tashi's head.

"Fight, fight, fight!" Chopper chanted enthusiastically, standing on a nearby chair.

Daisy stood next to them, watching the action. "Cute!" she exclaimed. She pulled a strand of hair from behind her ear and dipped the end into a jar of pink paint. It had been a long time since Daisy had fainted.

"Ladies, ladies. *Please* settle down," Ms. Heart pleaded from the front of the class. "You're supposed to paint a portrait of your face on the *canvas*, not paint your actual face! If you don't stop your shenanigans now, I'm going to—" Ms. Heart paused, and picked up the thick leatherbound book that lay open on her desk. Most of the bright-silver lettering on the spine had worn off from use, and the corners of the pages were dog-eared. "Well, I don't know what I'm going to do, but it involves a lesser grade or punishment of some sort. I think."

Gloria took another peek at the completed self-portrait on her canvas. It didn't look like anyone else's. Energetic strokes of yellow paint swirled next to a boisterous line of pink, and ecstatic dots of blue lined the edges. The painting, in Gloria's opinion, felt full of possibility. *This looks just like me*, Gloria thought, satisfied. Yup, the image on the canvas looked just how Gloria felt.

Across the hallway, Greta fidgeted at her desk. Mrs. Hastam's lecture about the little-known vulnerabilities of the Viking shield wall had lost its excitement, especially since Aisha insisted on raising her hand to ask questions. Everyone else in class just interrupted when they had something to say. Interruptions were much less time-consuming.

Finally, the bell, just a perfectly normal bell, rang. (The bloodcurdling scream bell was no more, thank goodness.) Class was over at last.

"Don't forget that basketball sign-ups are next week. I encourage everyone to come out and play!" Mrs. Hastam had taken over as the Gemini Academy basketball coach. Turned out her passion for history helped her avoid many tactical mistakes that had been made in the past.

"You think you can stop me this season, Garcia?" Lola taunted, rubbing her hands together.

"You think you can stop *me*?" Greta said as she put her notebook into her backpack.

"Oh, Garcia," Lola said, throwing her arm around Greta's shoulder. "You and your sister are so alike."

"Why, thank you," Greta said, smiling. That was the best compliment she could ever receive.

Twins poured out of the classrooms and into the hallway. Gloria and Greta found each other at once. Some students raced to their next class, and some students walked. Some students wore yellow shorts with a blue top, some wore a blue top with yellow shorts, and plenty of others wore monochrome outfits. All displayed chains around their necks with matching, shapeless, pearly stones. All except the young newbies; they were charm-free. The charms were now considered vintage, officially from a bygone era.

Gemini Academy was extra buzzy that afternoon. The annual Gemini Academy Fair—now referred to as *Omnes Geminae* (OG for short)—was only one day away. In accordance with the theme, Better Together, a joint committee of ex–Sun Twins and ex–Moon Twins led by Mrs. Hastam and Ms. Heart executed the pre-fair logistics. The event promised to be grand, innovative, and extravagantly decorated. There were even rumors of a mural!

"Hey, Daisy, wait up!" Lola called, weaving her way through the throngs of twins to catch up to Daisy, who was a few paces ahead. "You finish your math homework? I need the answer to number five."

"You can't copy my homework, Lola Lewis! I do not endorse cheating of any kind!"

"I'm not trying to cheat, jeez. Seriously, can you help me? I don't understand geometry at all. It's so . . . particular."

"Why don't you ask your sister?" Daisy whined.

"Because she's still mad I beat her in HORSE yesterday," Lana taunted, coming up from behind them. Lana flashed a toothy smile while Lola deliberately looked away. Lola was still a bit of a sore loser.

"Fine, but you owe me," Daisy said begrudgingly.

Greta and Gloria rolled their eyes and continued down the hallway. Together, they walked toward Ms. Joy's classroom (they had Botany 201: Flower Power!) behind Sierra and Mitten, who chatted excitedly as they walked.

"Hey, Sierra, where's Sharkbite?" Gloria realized she hadn't seen the snake in a while. Though the reptile had never sprouted fangs, he'd grown impossible to miss; last she saw him he was nearly the length of Sierra's arm, way too big to hold in the palm of her hand or to rest on her shoulder.

"Wild hearts must be set free," Sierra said wistfully. "And my dear Sharkbite had the wildest heart of all."

"Don't mind her," Mitten teased. "Anyway, so the mural wall for OG finally got approved! Ms. Heart is going to donate tons of paint. It's going to be massive. I'm thinking we'll do it right below the Gemini crest by the front entrance."

"Sweet," Gloria and Greta said in unison.

"I'm going to paint a picture of Sharkbite as my contribution to the piece," Sierra said deliberately. "So he knows he's not forgotten."

"Whatever you say, sis," Mitten said, good-naturedly.

Suddenly, the lights went dark, thunder clapped outside,

and the windowpanes jittered. A small colony of bats swarmed down the hallway. Or was it butterflies? Or both? Nevertheless, everybody groaned. This still happened from time to time. A few seconds later, the lights returned, revealing a thick cobweb that stretched across the hallway. The girls ducked underneath it, and continued on their way.

Yup, even a year later, Gemini Academy was still a little wonky.

Before the sun rose the next morning, Gloria and Greta met at the edge of the woods, ten paces past top-hat rock. It was Fraturday, after all—time for some sisterly bonding. Just as they had done every Fraturday for the past year, and every Fraturday for seven years before that. Lake Vetiti was no longer forbidden, but they still had to sneak. Gemini Academy students still weren't allowed out after curfew. That was one of the few rules that had stayed the same.

Greta arrived first, as usual. Her body concealed behind a tree, she poked her head out and peeked at the main castle while she waited for her sister. She was still getting used to the academy's new look. The vines that grew up the stone sides of the building were nearly obscured by a sprawling patch of multicolored wildflowers. Turned out the gas from all the old BLASTketballs was excellent fertilizer; the wildflower population was thriving. *Pretty*, Greta thought. The Gemini Academy crest remained above the entrance to the school.

Sometimes it looked more like a sun, and others it looked more like a moon. Tonight, Greta observed, it looked like equal bits of both.

"You're late," Greta said when Gloria arrived.

"Always," Gloria answered with a wink. "Let's go."

Together, they raced through the woods, not stopping until they reached the water's edge. They paused for a moment and wiggled their toes in the silky, pearly sand before diving head-first into the water.

The lake water was still the perfect temperature (refreshing, but not chilly) and the air smelled exactly the way that air should smell (pine trees and honeysuckle).

Greta floated on her back while Gloria treaded water next to her. Gloria still wasn't much of a floater. Their charms twinkled in the moonlight. For a long time neither sister spoke, instead choosing to enjoy the final moments of the deep, blue night in peaceful silence.

"Love you, twin," Greta whispered.

"Love you back, twin."

They reached for each other's hands and smiled and gazed upward. The sky was filled with stars.

ACKNOWLEDGMENTS

A gigantic thank-you to all the fine folks at Scholastic who had a hand, whether large or small, in building this book from beginning to end: David Levithan, Maeve Norton, Kerianne Okie, Duryan Bhagat-Clark, Maya Frank-Levine. And most of all, thank you to my editor, Orlando Dos Reis. From art logs to BLASTketball, you have been a most excellent leader every step of the way. Thank you for giving me this shot.

Thanks be to the endlessly generous Warner-Ryans, the original Sun and Moon Twins. Marja, I couldn't have done it or laughed that hard without you. I am still your biggest fan. Thank you.

I've been very fortunate to study with amazing instructors. Ann Hood, Coe Booth, and T. Geronimo Johnson all encouraged me to use my voice and taught me, in their own ways, how to find freedom within structure. A megathanks to Tor Seidler for a tremendous amount of support and encouragement; from you I learned the true meanings of accountability and specificity.

Thank you to my Writing for Children cohort for critiquing my work with honesty and heart since 2015. A special spotlight on the ultimate writing, reading, and sports-watching pal, Megan O'Brien: I am endlessly grateful for the hours you've spent giving me feedback, for listening, and for always responding to my most panicked texts.

I am surrounded by dear friends who have the uncanny ability to light my heart on fire with joy and laughter. Silva and my Bones. My ATL girls. I am so very lucky to have y'all in my corner. And you, Tim, thank you for lending your unguarded, one-of-a-kind whimsy.

And, of course, my hilarious, generous, and treasured family: Thank you. Momma, Dad, and Ham: the ultimate playmates and my very favorites. I love you all more than every star. Y'all keep my heart full.

ABOUT THE AUTHOR

Jessie Paddock holds a BFA in Drama from NYU's Tisch School of the Arts and an MFA in Writing for Children from The New School. She has lived in New York City for a while now, although she sometimes still misses her hometown of Atlanta. She loves to play soccer and ride her bike to places she's never been. This is her first novel.